THE LAZARUS EXPERIMENT

THE LAZARUS EXPERIMENT

Mark DeGasperi

THE LAZARUS EXPERIMENT

DOUBLE DRAGON

PROLOGUE

January 15, 2084

Where were her kids?

She wanted Cassie and Billy to see their father for breakfast when he woke up. He'd been commuting to Hong Kong and who knew what other places trying to drum up investments for their stricken area of New York State. In the kitchen, she cracked two eggs into a pan with butter and sank two pieces of rye bread into the toaster. She saw through the window that the latticework of ice on the Hudson River was hatcheted apart in last night's rainstorm. Her two children went out to play on the riverbank.

She heard a scream. She ran to the back door. The nine and eleven year olds in their parkas came bounding up the back lawn, what looked like ruptured earth pounded overnight then re-frozen. Cassie was wailing. Billy struggled to keep up with his older sister.

"Mommy!" her daughter cried.

She knelt to grab Cassie's shoulder at the door as Cassie puckered her face with disgust and held out her hands. In her mittens sat what appeared to be drenched black human hair. It was threaded through the eye sockets of a human skull.

She phoned the police. In minutes, she observed a two-man gyrocopter descend on the riverbank. On the street, a baby-faced cop waved away a news van from their home. Four-fifths of this block had moved away in the last year anyway, and the houses around them stood abandoned, dingy and unsellable. She watched police officers

5

trudging from the scene in front of her house. A ravaged-looking, old woman in a doorway across the street seemed to snap emotionally. She shrieked hysterically and wouldn't stop. Another breakdown. Everything was dreadful.

The young mother watched as the cops carried something they dredged from the Hudson. She spotted three skeletal fingers, like two were chewed off, which hung twig-like from the hammock. Snagged on a bone was a golden bracelet with a cursive letter "M." It looked expensive, she thought.

CHAPTER 1

Four days earlier, nearby:

The first thing he noticed was that there were no trees on his block, as though it had been bulldozed and repaved. Hadn't there been trees? Jonathan Kelton gazed at this through eyes that weren't real. He emerged from the car to view his three-story house, a dirty aquamarine stucco. Dr. Oskar Rose lifted him from the car. The doctor's shaved head gleamed in the late afternoon half-light. Rolls of fat rippled over a leather belt, sleeves of his white shirt rolled, cobalt blue tie loose; eyes dark and inscrutable. "Home," the doctor said.

Diana ran out the front door. A head shorter than he was and two years younger, round-faced and bright-eyed, she looked immaculately coiffed, ready to greet him, her natural strawberry-blond hair dropping to her shoulders in ringlets. She kissed him and he saw that her hand shook. A freckle-faced boy peeked out of the doorway then ran to him. He dropped to a squatting position to take the boy in his arms. Dr. Rose muttered a few words to Diana that he couldn't hear.

"Daddy," the boy said, breathless.

"My God, Henry. You've grown up, my little man."

Rose gave a wave then vanished into his car wordlessly. Diana led Jonathan into the house. Inside, a small banner stretched along the wall proclaiming in crayon, "Welcome back, Daddy."

7

Bleary, he tried to act relaxed and clear at least for his son's sake, as Diana spread out pillows for them to sit on the floor. Diana said, "So, you know, Henry just turned seven."

"Hey, happy birthday!" he said, feeling even more awkward acknowledging something this way that he should have remembered right away. He caught Henry staring at him, mouth slightly open. He knew he was emaciated and pale, though otherwise had been reassured he looked somewhat the same as before. At thirty-eight, he'd maintained a lean physique though now his very bones felt rubbery. He literally wore new skin. He looked outside, half-expecting his backyard to be split by a liver-colored gash where his lab used to be. Now, there was a patio.

It was then he realized he could barely remember actually working in his lab at all. Why should that be?

How broken was he, still?

"I want to hear about everything, buddy," he said to Henry. "All about school, everything. Since I've been away."

Of the approximate year he was gone, he'd only been fully conscious for the last few weeks. Diana had been allowed to visit him once, though not Henry, right before he was released. He'd remained bedridden. He'd been overjoyed to open his eyes and see her.

Sitting upright, now, he felt dizzy and his whole body ached - a vague, dull ache.

Diana brought out green tea and Henry's small, partially eaten chocolate birthday cake. "You look great," she told Jonathan.

8

"Even better, right?"

"Want to see a mirror?"

The last time he'd looked at himself was this morning before leaving the clinic, it was safe. "Bring it on."

She left the room and returned with a hand mirror. "See?" She placed a finger gently on a cleft in his chin. "Tender?"

"A little." The technology was amazing, he thought, as he gazed into his own blue eyes, the lids, the lashes. And this despite the fact that the neuroplastic devices they'd sunk into his skull like so many pipes weren't alive but did have the melding properties of living tissue. Soon, they'd be part of his body. The difference was they were durable enough to last a thousand years, his doctor had said, proudly; so, when his body decayed, Jonathan figured his new eyes and ears would be poking curiously through a husk of gristle.

From his cross-legged position on the floor, Henry said, "Are you good now, Daddy?"

"Oh, yeah."

"Kiddo," Diana said, sounding anxious, "Maybe Daddy should rest a little."

"Yeah, I…" She was right, he was enervated from doing nothing.

She silently directed Henry to take hold of his arms and lift him as though he couldn't do it himself. He pulled away gently to stand straight. He said, "See? Don't sweat it. A new man."

His son gave him a kiss before heading to his room. Not long after, Diana stretched out in their bed. Her eyes looked strangely backlit now, he thought, the iris with almost a neon glow. Whatever she'd taken made her more relaxed. He wouldn't bring it up now. Things were OK. All he had to do was get more mentally acute, he told himself.

"You look beautiful as ever," he said, meaning it, or wanting to mean it.

She beamed.

"Diana?… I think I'm having trouble remembering things."

"What do you mean? You know us, you know your home, you know everything."

"No. I don't know what happened to me."

He knew he'd been working on ordinary commercial chemical pesticides. He'd been credited with the first fool proof mosquito repellent to be taken internally. He built the home lab to refine the formula on commission so it could fight off all the stinger-equipped members of the insect population. His doctor acknowledged that there had been a mistake he made while working but Jonathan couldn't pinpoint it in his own mind. His most current records were destroyed in the sudden incineration of his lab so no one could say for sure what it was. There were volatile substances there that could be used for insect eradication. So why had no cause of the fire been determined? The debris was quickly cleared away and no one probed for a specific chemical signature, he'd been told. His body had absorbed different noxious substances. The priority, the only concern, they told him, was saving him. Dr. Rose didn't want him to think about it. Dr. Rose didn't give him any answers.

He might have to be satisfied that all he could know right now was that if he'd remained in the wreckage of the lab any longer, his body would not have been salvageable. Rose stepped in to claim his blind earthworm form. He knew that the doctor persuaded Diana to sign papers that allowed procedures for which his newly formed department at the Bluestone Clinic would absorb the cost.

"Does that even matter, Jon?" Diana asked.

"Why would you say that?"

"Why would I say that? Because I'm your wife who's glad you're home in one piece."

"But - what'd I do?"

"Well... You barely talked to me about your work."

"Then - I wish to God I had."

"At that time, we weren't talking too much."

"What? Were we fighting? Over what?"

"No, not fighting. There was just some, maybe... distance."

"Well, then... Couldn't have been important if I can't remember." He tried to make this sound light-hearted though it wasn't.

She said, "Be with Henry tomorrow after school, he needs that."

"Of course, of course. I want to... That was a little rough I guess, just now, sorry."

"No. You just have to become acclimated, the doctor said that... I did some things to the house. Hope you like them."

"I will, I'm sure." But he couldn't be sure he would know the difference. Didn't she realize that was what he was trying to tell her?

What he understood at this point - continuing a mental list of what he did know - was that the barrier between his lab and the house had stood in

11

place. It was why the fire hadn't spread; why their home wasn't harmed.

He said, "Anyway, something must've happened out here while I was inside the clinic. When we were driving here, everything seemed just... dead, no flora at all. Rose didn't give me access to news either."

"Maybe tomorrow or the next day you can look at the news. That'll tell you things. Nothing to worry about now."

"I worry about not knowing."

She stared at the ceiling and smiled. "Well, that sounds like the same old Jonathan."

"I know it'll go away but right now I don't like this feeling of - of, you know, disarrangement."

She sighed. "You're impossible."

"Well?"

"Everything's all right now... Some jerk set off an eco-bomb."

"Eco-bomb! I..." He didn't know where to begin with that. "Who, do they know?"

"A local kid, unemployed... Used to be a science student."

"Where?"

"Actually, from Kingston."

She meant the State University there - his own college. "You're kidding."

She caressed his cheek. "Yes, you married me for my sense of humor... You are thinking too much."

"Tell me when."

"When? Last year."

"Just to make sure," he said, only half-joking, "the year is 2084?"

"You don't have to keep second guessing things. It's January 11."

"Diana... please let me know everything. I can't relax until I do."

She sighed again and tapped a keypad by the bed. The wall screen lit up and indeed told him things he could barely stand to hear.

13

CHAPTER 2

Images of a cornfield dewy in morning haze shifted back and forth in wide pans. Someone was walking briskly down an empty country road wearing an "eyebeam," a corneal insert that worked as a camera. The audience was seeing whatever this person was. Far off, clouds looked cottony in a windy blue sky. There was the sound of a distant explosion. It seemed like the full moon lit up for a second, or like a big, peering eye boring through a cloud. The person with the eyebeam ran towards this sight to catch it on tape. When the cloud parted, a small plane roared into view. But the plane went off in two different directions. It had blasted in two. The cockpit half did a somersault and plunged in a downward loop then vanished from view. Only the rapid breath of the person with the eyebeam could be heard and vague mutterings of shock.

Quiet descended over the cornstalks. A man darted breathlessly out from this field from the other side. He was a farm laborer, weathered and middle-aged.

"The hell was that?" eyebeam-man asked, unseen from behind the camera.

"I don't know," the farmhand answered. He looked into the robotic eye that captured his image then back at the horizon.

Eyebeam-man said, "I heard a weird noise, that plane was flyin' too low. No planes around here. Never."

Silence between them for a moment, only the arrhythmia of their breathing.

"That guy in the plane did some shit," the other man said.

"What do you mean?"

"Somethin'."

"Blew himself up is what."

"Fuck no, somethin'. Somethin' came outta the back of the plane." This man's craggy face seemed to freeze, stone-like.

"How you feelin', chief?" eyebeam-man asked.

"All right," he said. Then, spastically, "Yeah, I, all right…"

The farm guy bent forward and retched. Blood gushed from his mouth and panicked eyebeam-man didn't know where to look, his gaze shooting up and down. It came to rest on what looked like a rancid, pulpy tomato on the asphalt. It looked like the man vomited up half of his stomach.

Then came screams from eyebeam-man with images bouncing up and down as he ran. A reddish tinge crept into the edges of the video frame. His own blood. Until the camera view flipped sideways to stare into the cornfield and just stay there. Eyebeam-man had collapsed in the road and this was the last thing his living eye saw.

A time lapse occurred. After this man's death, the videotape had been speeded up for public viewing. The reddish images blurred. The cornstalks shriveled into fleshy sticks, which buckled on top of each other and collapsed. This happened in a matter of days, before the man's body was retrieved. The field that had stood six feet high became a prickly wasteland to the horizon.

This was nine months ago. This was the birth of "God-zero."

The lone terrorist attack got its name as analogous to the idea of "ground zero." That's what Jonathan heard on the news replay. But the site of detonation was in the sky, a mid-air chemical metastasis. There was no conflagration since it was an airborne bio-toxin. It was carried on the wind. To some pundits, it was as if a god sought punishment for mankind's hubris - or they thought that was the killer's intent. God-zero. What amounted to a morbidly ironic name for the event.

In this news montage, the scene shifted to the Hudson River under the Rip Van Winkle Bridge. It looked like the river had been paved with stones. These were dead fish.

Diana shut the TV off. "Enough, OK?"

"Jesus Christ."

"Satisfied?" She looked at him in bed. "Now you know about as much as we all do."

After the attack, whole nearby towns were wiped out. Outlying ones were evacuated, many inhabitants never to return.

The final death toll: 323,115.

It was James Martinson, age 27, who had set it off over the Hudson Valley. He seemed to be a science graduate who was rebelling against science, if his actions could be accorded any logic. He was showing how it could be destructive - while destroying the modern world at the same time. In his twisted way, maybe he was a Luddite. He sent poison raining down by light aircraft. He killed himself in his plane in the process. Eventually, his

16

insidious but scattershot creation was mostly contained.

Jonathan knew that the potential for something like this was one of the reasons counties in New York a decade ago had been combined into Cantons, to consolidate power within decentralized units. So much for that. But if Martinson made demands or left a statement or manifesto, government sources snapped it up and it was hidden away. The information glut of earlier decades had long ended. Information was power and it was getting harder to come by for everyday people.

So in the end, really, nobody knew why he did it.

What an extraordinary thing to have happened during the past year, and so close to home, he thought; a time in which he experienced his own personal devastation.

Diana said, "Look, I was only supposed to try to talk about... about positive things."

"OK, sweetheart." She was trying as best she could to make him feel better in this almost impossibly distressed new environment.

"No more news. That's it. You just got to relax. All right?"

"OK." In a second, he said, "I love you."

"Oh, Jon. I love you too."

She kissed his cheek and left the room.

In a minute, he caught sight on the dresser of a notebook. It must have been placed there for him by Diana. He flipped back the metallic cover. Pages lay before him with plastic pockets containing washer-sized disks, arranged chronologically, his class records from the

University of Kingston. He slipped disc after disc in a cuticle ridge in the notebook, which projected class lists, grades and written examinations, perusing them quickly. These seemed mundane.

One particular roster, from the semester before the fire, the last class he'd taught before his sabbatical, compelled him. He stared at it. Frustratingly, astonishingly, none of these names meant anything to him.

He couldn't think about any of these things now.

Too much.

He dropped heavily into a well of sleep. But it wasn't for long.

CHAPTER 3

In bed alone, he jolted awake - as if underwater, starving for air, thrusting to the surface and into bright sunlight -

He's lying on damp grass, sapphire sky above. A girl's moon-white face hovers over him. Pouty lips. Purple lipstick.

She undoes the buttons of a loose-fitting, collared white shirt. Alabaster breasts tumble out with stunningly bulbous, deep plum-red nipples. His breath catches. He knew their relationship would spill into this; felt it would happen today for the first time, here. A breeze stirs, giving wings to her own scent, somehow spicy like thyme and roses mixed with the fresh earth smell. Her stringy black hair windily curtains her breasts.

Expectation and reality collide in a fireburst in his belly. She slips him into her, achingly sweet.

She says his name in a low voice, Jonathan. She grunts, throaty and aggressive, almost feral.

He closes his eyes and yells out her name, Mitcha -

In a second, she says, I'm scared...

His eyes open, he reoriented himself to his bedroom. He sat up with effort, weirdly ashamed, with the glaring clarity of that recollection, like exposure.

Mitcha. Who was she? When and where was that -?

I'm scared...

19

This came to him as he was awakening. He wondered if it was a memory, not some fantasy dream; at a point he'd been hungry for memories. Was that so?

Maybe. Wow, he thought. He made himself stop thinking about it. Stop thinking about everything. This was nonsense.

There was nothing else he could think, nothing else he could remember, about her.

In the shower off the master bedroom, a steamy mist rained from the ceiling as he sat on a mock-marble bench, letting it kiss his body. The arching, white-columned room offered a Jacuzzi and sunroom, the gilded bathroom facilities lying behind a curtain of electric blue light. He was careful with the way he touched his own frame. The doctor said that whatever minimal scarring existed after all the skin fusion would heal - and he was still mostly real flesh and blood, even if all transfused, the doctor assured him. Real flesh, he kept reminding himself of that. There was simply a reshaping going on, a settling in. His epidermis hurt mildly but without localized pain, like he'd gotten a sunburn across his whole body.

In minutes, sitting on the bed in his bathrobe, he accessed his old messages that scrolled down the wall screen, fragmented text and voices. There weren't many, given he'd been gone almost a year; not even a dozen, most with office numbers instead of home numbers.

No one named Mitcha had tried to contact him.

He returned to the class list from the semester before the fire in his lab. A name popped out at him from his graduate chemistry course: Mitcha Ebrey.

20

He'd gazed at it earlier. He hadn't recognized it then. But subliminally he must have.

Maybe it was what propelled the images.

He called up the girl's i.d. photo. Smiling, she looked like an innocent teen, no lipstick, her hair different, shorter and a tawnier shade.

But it was the girl from his mind. She was real.

CHAPTER 4

He felt a sense of unanticipated urgency keeping his first appointment with his doctor. He barely knew Dr. Rose and hadn't particularly warmed to him, Jonathan considered, as he slipped on a too-loose, metallic-looking, peacock blue thermal jacket that Diana bought for him. He looked in the mirror with the uncomfortable thought that he seemed some contracted semblance of himself, almost an elegant shrunken head.

More nonsense. He was real flesh. He was himself. He would repeat that like a mantra.

Before God-zero erupted last year, Dr. Rose, who happened to have taught at the same university Jonathan did, opened the Bluestone Clinic as his own private research facility. The doctor had urged him to try to get on with a normal life and was intent on avoiding a clinical environment for their meeting. Jonathan learned from Diana that one place they'd frequented with Henry was the Starburst Automat close by. At 5 PM, Henry had enjoyed blueberry pancakes with the maple syrup that once came from local farms. Rose told him to pick a place where he felt comfortable so he settled for this. From afar, as he drove closer, the diner, squared off by intersecting empty streets, looking like a gigantic slab of ice. The shiny metallic, powder blue tinted walls made it impossible to see in. It was unpartitioned and tiered, a warehouse of a restaurant, with tables that resembled carved chunks of agate. Only two people, what looked like father and son, he thought, sat at the other side of the place, lit by separate lights like on a stage. Otherwise, it was empty.

He sat in a booth and stuck a credit card into a slit. A four-foot circle in the mirror-like floor flew open. An automaton with a softly curved female figure arose, her uniform a thousand gold sequins, her face mannequin-like. Her cheeks looked like congealed grease. "Good afternoon," she said, in a child-like voice.

"Café latte," he said.

She descended into the floor, which sealed behind her. The automat offered novelty appeal like some cheap theme park exhibit. He could see why his little son liked it. In seconds, the server reappeared and with a pasty white hand placed a china cup of frothy coffee before him with a cinnamon stick. The menu listings glowed on the tabletop, specials floating forward three-dimensionally. He could order without saying a word but said, "I'm waiting for someone."

Her fuchsia button-eyes blinked and she smiled. She disappeared into the great underneath. He got a whiff of rotting vegetables. He didn't really want the coffee and the smell momentarily made him feel ill. Rose walked in, footsteps echoing in the large room.

"How's this place for you?" Jonathan asked him.

"How is it for you?"

"Wonderful."

Jonathan forced himself to take a sip of coffee for the caffeine boost, he was allowed. He also wanted the doctor to feel at ease, so he could get information. "Maybe you should have something. My son likes the blueberry pancakes."

"I might or might not." Rose's speech patterns sounded somewhat affected, a nasal tone, a measured voice; in some sense imperious, in contrast to his appearance. "You go ahead," Rose said.

"I don't want anything." Meeting here suddenly seemed all the more absurd. "But I would like to talk to you."

"Something troubles you."

"I'm experiencing some kind of retrograde amnesia. There are these - gaps, or holes."

Rose asked, "Is there normal retention of day to day events? Is there any common forgetfulness in the present?"

"I don't think so, not so far... I remember the distant past ... I've thought about things. Henry's birth on Long Island, moving up here, starting the job at the college but..."

"Well, you've concluded yourself that concussive impact to your forebrain might have caused some post-traumatic amnesia."

"Yes. But maybe unusual, though, to experience it in this way, when no symptoms otherwise?"

"Unusual isn't the word, Jonathan. We're in a new realm of understanding and diagnoses. I can tell you that there are no detectable aberrations. Are you in pain?"

"No. Thank you, I do appreciate that. But... I'd just like to get those recent memories back. You know?"

"Well. It's not something I can do," Rose said. "To the extent that bits of memory are physical, organic, they simply may be gone. As you know, your brainstem, thankfully for you, was not so damaged. That's one of the reasons there was a chance for such reconstruction. But your brain suffered both intense impact and heat."

"Well... Right now, it's confusing for me, doctor, confusing and a little frightening."

"Just let yourself recover. Like coming here and enjoying this place, for example."

"I'm not enjoying this place." He took a deep breath and admitted to himself too, "Or... practically anything in the right way."

Rose stared at him for a second. "It's self-correcting, Jonathan." Now, he sounded exasperated.

"What do you mean by 'self-correcting?' Something other than natural healing? What?"

Rose pursed his lips.

"Come on, I'm a scientist too," Jonathan said. "Not just your patient."

It took the doctor a moment before he said, "All right. Come with me. But please don't challenge me again."

CHAPTER 5

They entered the doctor's car, parked right outside the automat. It was ambulance-red and white and stretch-limo long, a pair of slits opening over a chrome grill in front like a pair of suspicious eyes. Within, the windowless, driverless vehicle stared into itself with a cloudy sea-green eyeball from the angled red velvet roof so it kept watch on its passengers as well as the road. The doctor murmured a few numbers within this his mobile office. A back wall of the car lit up as a holographic projection streamed through a thin rain of water vapor from the ceiling to create a screen. Jonathan found himself gazing into a freezer-like rectangle of a chamber. The sole illumination poured from a suspended, revolving body, transparent, organs, blood vessels and brain exposed. Like a living autopsy.

He fell back. He saw Dr. Jonathan Kelton staring back at him. His own face. "Jesus."

"Your secondary neural network, if you will. At the Bluestone Clinic. A safety net. Yes, it's good that you know."

"A coldcell." He blurted this out. He retained this knowledge - of a chip implant no larger than a human cell: Rose had put a coldcell in his head.

The doctor said, "It monitors all your body functions, all your necessary medical data for interface. It's invisible, painless and requires no maintenance by you, no outerware. You should be pleased."

Jonathan scratched a line of skin on the back of his hand. He winced as he watched the hand of the matching Jonathan sprout a red weed. Light danced in the eye sockets.

"What are you trying to prove by that?"

"That it's even more than what you said. I can figure that out, doctor."

Rose took a deep breath and called out another code. The globule and the electric effigy of himself it contained appeared to evaporate.

Jonathan said, "The eye and ear implants - you can see and hear what I do through them. That's why almost as soon as I became aware you were able to release me from the clinic. You're inside me."

"That's not the way we look at it. But sensory input is transmitted, yes."

"No, meaning, you're living my life with me. Somebody somewhere get some voyeuristic thrill out of it?"

"Nobody's watching what you say and do. It's strictly to pick up anomalies. Potential external or internal dangers." He frowned. "You as a scientist should accept that."

"No, I refuse."

"I beg your pardon?"

"I'm lucid. My body's functioning. It's amazing, I know it is. But I'd rather not have that thing inside me."

"Given the opportunity of maximum oversight, we took it. A patient needs to be able to go anywhere, what's the point otherwise? We didn't want to keep you confined to the clinic, that's what it would have been. Diana signed off on it."

27

"But I… When I speak to my son. Or if - if I make love to my wife… this is recorded!"

"We're not spying on you in that way… Anyway, it can possibly be temporary."

"Only temporary? How long?"

"Eight months? One year? Depends partly on you. Right now, I'm sorry to say your attitude isn't helping."

"I have free will." There was defiance in his voice.

"I don't know exactly what you mean."

"You can't - you wouldn't - control me in some way."

"Please don't be foolish. This involves your convalescence. Unimpeded and healthful."

Jonathan looked out one of the car's window slats. They hadn't left the parking lot. He watched a young couple and their two little kids enter the Automat. Diana said they'd had fun here too yet he hadn't even known where it was. He thought of something else, now. "Is it interfering? The coldcell. That's why I'm having the memory lapses. Couldn't it be that there's some kind of blocking going on, short-circuiting, even if not intended by you?"

"Well… I don't know."

"Doctor, don't tell me you don't know. What else was done?"

The doctor watched him for a moment. They stared each other down. "Well, naturally, what was most conducive to your healing was to delete the moment of trauma."

"Wait a minute, you're telling me you purposely erased the memory of the fire? You could do that?"

"As your most prominent, most powerful and recent memory, we were able to disenable the retrieval process, yes. Again, you should be pleased and grateful."

"You took that away from me so I'd never know how the accident actually happened?"

"This is not about information retrieval. This is eliminating the memory of devastating pain from the body."

"So in the process of your doing that, I'm forgetting other things as well?"

"Absolutely not. You've come back home as if nothing happened. Damn it. Concentrate on the present, not the past. Why must you be so resistant?"

"All right," Jonathan said, finally. "Yes, you're right, of course."

He couldn't argue anymore - there was nothing he could argue about. But what was new and strange inside him seemed at quiet war with his ego. He didn't expect to feel like a foreigner in his own skin and now, so randomly exposed; with his heartache, his humiliation, everything, reduced to algorithms.

He felt determined to reconstruct his past, which only he could do. No matter what he might learn.

CHAPTER 6

Without another word, Rose let him out into the wasteland of the parking lot in the low, cold glare of the sun.

This girl Mitcha Ebrey remained the only individual outside his family that he remembered immediately.

There seemed no reason to bring her up specifically to his doctor. His incandescent recollection of her - assuming it was a recollection - seemed tawdry and maybe even a professional and personal embarrassment. Also, at the moment, he felt nothing for this girl - she was like a stranger to him. But how could he dismiss that unsettling, highly charged sexual scene in his head? Could his marriage have bracketed it?

She lived in him somehow. Maybe she would come back into his life, he considered; maybe that would be damaging and he'd have to try to prevent it; or maybe it wouldn't but she could tell him things about himself that no one else could. So it was worth at least trying to find out more about her, he convinced himself. A phone number for her from his university records was no longer in service, he'd looked into that discreetly at home. Now, sitting outside the diner in his own corn-green, nine year old Ford Roguebat, he did more research. All her credits that he could pull up in the car were slight academic ones. Her writing in some minor scientific publications, unremarkable and not revelatory, was years old. He checked to see if she could have perished in God-zero. Her name was not among the victims.

He knew that she studied climatology at his one-time campus, the State University at Kingston, at the time he taught there. So he returned to the college for the first time since getting out of the clinic. His vehicle still held his security pass so, after brief questioning by a guard, he was allowed to proceed through the main gate of the State University. He'd had maximum clearance. The ten-story bunker-like building of the Graduate Research Center, painted sea-blue, loomed before him, strange and familiar at the same time like in a dream.

In the Climatology Department, a two hundred-foot diorama of world weather greeted him with its ever-changing dreamscape of an ocean of air and its dark sub-streams. The vast hall sat empty, though in a separate room off the diorama rotunda, he spotted an old woman bent over consoles. At a glance, he could guess her age to be about a hundred and thirty, her days prolonged but her body seemingly left without resonance.

"Excuse me," he called to her, his voice echoing. She moved to look at him as if in slow motion. "I'm Dr. Kelton. Worked in Biochem."

"Koblensk. Rainwater samples."

"I was wondering if anybody knew where a student named Mitcha Ebrey was."

"It's not my business what a young girl does," she said.

He was unexpectedly both relieved and excited. "So you do know her?" Still, maybe it wasn't his business either.

"Not anymore." The woman's fingers went to her keyboard like a battery of destabilized missiles, as a dozen vials of water - pink, lime-green, burgundy - clicked by her. "She was working on the storm tide models."

"Of what?"

"The Northeast Atlantic coast. And the Hudson. Fairly ordinary work."

"When was the last time she was here?"

The woman threw up a hand towards a round protuberance, its glass eye fixed ceilingward. "Check the usage roster." He walked to the device. Koblensk moved closer to him, eyes narrowing as if he were a specimen coming into focus on a glass slide. "You've been burned."

"Yes. In my lab."

"I was burned. But only on the inside. I shouldn't have survived but I did. There was no burning feeling. It felt, on the skin, like summer rain. Gentle. And inside, a sweet taste, like sugar in whisky. Hot and sweet. It was uncanny. Insidious. The children yelled, they didn't know what the taste was. The adults just didn't know what to do."

"Yes, God-zero, I'm sorry."

The old woman punched in a code for him. A voice told him, "December 19, 2082."

So Mitcha Ebrey hadn't been to the college since two months before his accident.

He said, "That was a while ago that she was here, she must be working somewhere, maybe at another institution."

32

"She dropped out of this program. If a student isn't interested herself, why would anyone pursue her?"

"What was she like?" he asked.

"Please leave me alone."

"So you don't know?" He sounded testy. He was taking his frustration out on her. "Look, I'm sorry. Nobody knows what happened to her?"

"Why are you pestering me now?" she said. "She just disappeared."

CHAPTER 7

He exited into a concrete pavilion under a grimy white dome, an eco-protective metal bubble over the college - new since he was last here, since God-zero - which was half-deserted for the winter break and looking God-forsaken. A button trembled on his collar and he flicked at it. It was Diana. "Hi."

"Hello, sweetheart. What are you doing?"

"Just looking up some old colleagues, let people know I'm OK."

"What did the doctor say?"

"I found out everything he did... I just - feel weird, Diana."

"I can understand. Come home."

"Yeah, I'm coming."

Before he hung up, he thought he heard her mumble, "Don't ruin everything." Possibly, he was mistaken.

He took in the world around him anew as he drove home. On a tract of gray land, flat from the edge of the road to the horizon, a series of doorways stood lined up. They looked like a string of portable toilets. A billboard advertised new condos. The inhabitants of this subterranean colony could drop to safe homes with fake vistas. He took a detour across the Kingston-Rhinecliff Bridge to see what had once been a Mid-Hudson shopping mall, which was an enclosed five square miles, twenty stories high. It sat abandoned. He drove past a McDonalds then a Burger King, shuttered, and a

KFC split in half, the building like big, broken, ashy teeth in the open wind. Many of the cars zipping past him seemed strange models, all self-guided in any case, with no traffic jams or need for traffic lights on the roads, and hurtling at up to two hundred miles an hour. In this nervous dusk, pale clouds, seemingly innocuous, which leaned on the edge of the sloping, dawn-blue mountains, might hide the hand of a poisoner, if God-zero, or one day, even worse toxins re-emerged.

Underneath were miles and miles of nothing.

The next morning, he awoke alone. Diana had driven Henry to school. In the bathroom, he popped a hormonal enhancer provided by Dr. Rose. He brushed back his sweat-stiffened hair and noticed it was getting unruly - the doctors had restored it to its roots after being seared to his skull. In the metal trash can in the bathroom he spotted a small subcutaneous patch. So Diana was taking something. He opened the top dresser drawers. Under her panties, he hit upon a vial labeled Eufonia.

Eufonia. The drug sounded familiar but he couldn't place it. He felt momentary anxiety. This must have been what accounted for her muted moods; why even her cheeriness sometimes seemed a little disengaged. He didn't understand why it disconcerted him, it shouldn't have. She'd been a medieval history major, with a biology minor - a gifted student. She was a part-time teacher before they moved from Long Island. But she'd been unemployed and alone with Henry this whole time upstate. Now, she was Jonathan's caregiver. He didn't know when she'd started taking it, but her trying to find relief in something like Eufonia was the least he could expect.

His notebook still lay on the bedside table. He went through his class lists again, scanning the projections. He fixed upon the name Mitcha Ebrey from that final class before his lab fire. Even if she was irrelevant, the process seemed less about her than the larger truth: objects produced psychological responses. It was cued recall. Could he hasten it?

Something else caught his eye: one student, Dunstan Booker, was in the same Fundamentals of Modern Chemistry class as Mitcha Ebrey. Dunstan was one of the names on Jonathan's call list, having left a message some months back. He couldn't think of the face to go with the name. He called out for Dunstan's message to be played back.

A high-pitched voice said, "Mrs. Kelton, this is Dunstan Booker, I was a student of your husband's. Just wanted to, uh, express my condolences."

He thought Jonathan was dead.

"Please let me know if there's anything I can do… Um, actually, I'm wondering if you could call me back anyway, got a question for you about your husband's work, if you can help me."

He checked the phone records. Diana never called Dunstan back, it looked like. She must have been barely functional for much of this time. He called out for the phone number and a male voice answered. "Hello?"

"This Dunstan?"

"Who's this?"

"Dr. Jonathan Kelton."

36

"Go fuck yourself, Santiago, you two-mamas' boy."

"Wait, Dunstan, it's me, the guy who gave you an A+. Two classes worth."

He switched the signal to project his visual image. He heard heavy breaths. A cherubic-looking, red-haired young man stepped out as if from a fold in the wall, wraith-like. "Wait, is this for real? Are you real?"

"Just got out of the hospital, after all this time. Here I am calling you back."

"Jeez, how do you feel?"

"OK, under the circumstances."

"Well, we gotta get together, have two or five 24-ounce brews. I'm working on cryogenics now, that's taking off. These hibernational utopians. Wanna go to sleep until a better world comes along. I'd like to pick your brain -" The view of Dunstan in blue boxer shorts switched off. "'Scuse me, gotta get dressed, you don't wanna see my boy swingin' in the cool breeze, though it is a remarkable sight."

"When you called, you said you had a question about me for my wife."

"Oh, yeah. Well, Professor, you remember that we talked a few weeks before the fire in your lab?"

"Not sure. You know anything about the fire in my lab, Dunstan?"

"What I'm wondering, is that you got the sanguivent from me -"

"Sanguivent."

"That serum -'blows' through the bloodstream as a potential immune booster. I know you never made tenure but I figure you could've been doing something worthwhile at least. Sorry, I mean I

37

don't know how close you got to realizing an analog."

"Not close, I don't think."

"What I'm interested in is combining it with some fluorocarbons, so we can turn people, like medically 'perfect' while their tissue is frozen cryogenically. Not only do you go to sleep for seven hundred years but you wake up in a perfect body. I think we could really do it."

"A little more than I can deal with right now."

"That's not my point. You ordered it through the department. I took the request. Your home lab was stocked with it."

"OK, Dunstan, I believe that. So?"

"Sanguivent isn't flammable. So there were a couple nights way back when I couldn't sleep, just trying to think about what kind of shit you were doing. There's no reason I could see, if that's what you were using, that your lab would blow up."

The air filtration unit kicked into high gear and chimes rang as the household sensors received a high-pollution alert. It would be safer to remain indoors or to carry a portable breathing device, he'd heard that on the news. Each member of the family had one in his or her own size, Henry's a multi-colored face like a Halloween mask, he'd seen.

He checked to see what records existed of what he'd ordered for his lab. His main inventory list had been destroyed. Whatever official documentation remained was in possession of his employer, the Wright Group. But if he'd made requests through the college, as Dunstan indicated, those might be separate. In the home database, in fact he found a

38

requisition form for sanguivent and he'd taken possession of two canisters.

He saw only one more order. He'd requested Kerosote through Kingston University. He read how Kerosote was a new and experimental chemical also being tested for eco-countermeasures; a low explosive with a shaped charge for a contained, concentric horizontal discharge, heated by a laser arc. He must have conjectured that in miniscule amounts it could be used in pinpoint bombs to deflagrate in mid-air, to descend in the midst of an invading swarm of predatory bugs. It would wipe them out. Of course, he didn't remember either order - they fell within his purview of missing time. Kerosote would have represented a departure from his experiments. In any case, it was a dangerous and restricted substance. The school had denied his request.

"Hey, I wonder if you can do me a favor," he said to Dunstan.

The young man popped back to life, looking harried. "Probably not. Depends. What?"

"Help me figure out why what should never have happened did happen."

CHAPTER 8

A little later, he navigated a winding street, driving past the rotted riverfront of burned-out and cannibalized buildings, where once, only five hundred years ago, the fertile plains and clear water of the Esopus Creek drew Dutch settlers.

He'd asked Dunstan to meet in an out of the way place, settling on this Rondout waterfront. The Biosphere had been constructed a decade ago as an eco-experiment, enough to hold a colony of a thousand people but it ran out of funds, its metal dome left to rust. It took on the look of a huge, burnt-out light bulb, blackened yellow-white, dropped into the middle of the dully gleaming, not long de-populated skyline of Kingston. It had been reconverted into a New Way church.

In the interim, before coming here, he'd phoned all the other names on his call list. There were no other students, these were academic and corporate well-wishers who'd found out that he was in the Bluestone Clinic but who barely knew him.

Inside the church, a cupola soared two hundred feet over him in a dreamy parabola with its own angels, translucent figures in white, like distant, circling snowbirds. The altar spread out like a house-sized clamshell of light. A glowing waterfall offered the illusion of pulling everyone in.

He found his former student in a pew. Dunstan said, "My folks brought me when it was called the Biosphere. Nobody really ever thought they would use it on Earth. Testing it for use on Mars, before we totally gave up the space program. But... no other life out there, right? If there hasn't been contact yet, why should there ever be? It didn't happen in the last billion years. That means it won't happen, it can't. We're all alone in this universe. No other life. Just us here on this pathetic little planet... Anyway, they thought people could live in this ratty place for generations. Right? Bullshit anyway."

"It would've worked, in the context of what was being proposed."

"Oh, OK. People can get used to anything, I guess, that's what you mean. You're living proof of it."

Jonathan said nothing. All alone on this pathetic little planet, he thought.

"Hey, I mean -"

"Forget it. Fact is, you can't really - you know, get used to anything."

"You think I can help you somehow, Professor? What's this about?"

Jonathan moved closer in the pew and slid over a sheaf of papers. The younger man perused them. "Diagnostics. That I can get at least. Part of my memory's gone."

"What's so pressing?"

"Well, my lab - everything gone, blown to hell and I don't know why, to start with. Nobody seems to know why."

"How could you not know?"

"I still have to get my inventory list. Meantime, I just found out I put in a request for Kerosote through the college but wasn't able to get it."

"I don't know anything about that," he said, a little nervously. "I don't want to be tagged with anything."

"No, no, that's not it. I'm saying that I also can't remember people I've known. People who might care about me, who I should be reaching out to."

"Wouldn't they contact you, now that you're home?"

What else could he tell Dunstan? About Mitcha Ebrey? It wasn't about her specifically, he told himself again, it was about all the gaps. "It's that I might not know them now. There are some things about my wife and child I don't even recall properly. But I do believe that some memories are still there unconsciously."

"Oh. I think I see what you're getting at. You want some kind of remote trigger. Like a mind-d."

"Yes." He knew that's what he wanted - a mind-d, d for diode. A uni-directional device that converted electricity into psychogenic energy; one designed for memory recovery.

"Aren't you worried that if you accidentally interfere with mister microchip, you'll fuck up the works?"

"Low power stimulus? It can't override the coldcell, that's way too powerful."

"They keep on with the coldcell, our brains will work a billion trillion times faster, no shit. If there's an information-acceleration cerebral merge. But can't get that, no way. Too expensive. Not available. Whatever."

"The coldcell I have is mainly a stabilizer, a medical monitor. Also, my doctor didn't want me

42

to relive the trauma of the lab fire in my head. So it had a memory application too. Fair enough. But now, this partial amnesia seems to be a secondary symptom. He says it's not but I know it is. So I wonder if I can treat it."

"You're nuts, you really think you can do it yourself?"

"How could I help but wonder if I can? Look, Dunstan, my doctor told me to get back to the semblance of a normal life. Well, I can't unless I remember things. Right?"

"Your doc's not interested in these memory problems of yours? He even caused them? That's your pitch?"

"Not his fault, of course. I'm looking for things that are beyond his purview... Fifteen billion nerve cells in the brain, right? Unknown valences. People talk about the physical organs all the time but can still hardly talk about the 'mind' with that kind of specificity. The different pieces never add up. Never explain how someone can reason. Or create. Love... Right?"

"I don't know. If I can get it - if I do it - I'll leave a package the same time tomorrow."

"Charge me what you need to."

"Dr. Kelton - you don't need me to tell you."

An angel whisked past in a flashbulb burst of light. "What?"

"Psychosurgery's calibrated down to femtometers. I'm not an electro-organic surgeon and neither are you. Make sure you don't wind up with the equivalent of a lobotomy. The ice pick through your eyeball that rips out a third of your brain."

43

"Come on, don't be silly. If used properly -"

"Properly? Say a psychotic grabs a mind, it might only reinforce their delusions."

He didn't know what to say to that. Did Dunstan think he was losing his mind?

Dunstan stood. Jonathan said, "Hey, listen, do you know anything about Mitcha Ebrey? She was in your class last year."

"Mitcha Ebrey? No, didn't really know her. Why would you ask that?"

"Well... I found out she stopped coming to school and I wondered why."

"Who knows? Who cares? I think she was more than a little bit chipped."

"What do you mean?"

"I don't think I said word one to her. But once she was sitting next to me in class and I looked over and her sleeve was rolled up and I saw scars. Looked like fresh scars. Like she'd taken a knife to herself. Or somebody else did."

CHAPTER 9

That thought kept coming back to him in the time it took to cruise up the driveway to the twenty-room house that belonged to his erstwhile boss Jared Wright. It was set back a mile from the road behind pines shaped like hoop dresses, blue spruce and sycamores, in neat rows. It was impossible that these trees had survived God-zero. They'd been transported here within the last several months. He pulled in front of Wright's white-columned, Georgian-style home.

Wearing a white shirt, gray blazer and neatly pressed slacks under his worn cashmere coat, he tried to reassure himself that he looked eminently employable. It didn't work. He felt anxious and something like creaky. He rang the bell, with musical chimes. A young blond woman in a chef's apron answered the door, taking his coat, and without a word ushered him through the dining room. This opened to the right with its twelve foot ceiling and imposing mahogany table. At a little after 2 PM, sunlight bathed this room, glaring off the burnished wood. A huge, garish oil painting of a Catskill Mountain sunrise seemed to explode on the wall. Next came the living room, with a crystal chandelier with glistening teardrop icing. A concert grand piano sat closed and neglected with no sheet music and an uncreased black leather couch stretched in an L-shape from the piano. He followed the young woman into a rear, sunken room with walls of floor-to-ceiling glass presenting a

45

view of the uniformly green back lawn, where the grass ended in a private dock on a narrow river canal.

Jared Wright stood before at fireplace mantle, tall and sunburned, his face the color of a pale tomato, white hair slicked back; looking youthful despite his eighty-nine years. He wore a floor-length, daisy yellow robe and onyx and turquoise necklace. "Hello there."

They shook hands. Wright's grip was firm. Jonathan said, "Hi, sir. I'm glad to see you in such good health."

"Likewise."

Jonathan forced a smile. "Yes, as you see, I'm recovered."

Wright craned his neck forward to look closer at him then tilted his head curiously. "Remarkable. The Bluestone Clinic."

"I have them to thank."

"Right down the road."

He didn't want to bring up the coldcell; that his doctor was also literally inside his head; nor that a clump of memory had been snatched away. He let himself absorb the sunny, airy tranquility of his surroundings. "Your home is lovely." He had no memory or record that he'd ever been here before.

"I refreshed the landscaping a little bit. Hah. Luckily for me I happen to have a bunker too. Twenty feet down. So I was able to avoid all that mess. Family OK?"

"They're great." As far as he knew, Wright himself was estranged from his ex-wife and children in California. Jonathan said, "I think it's time for us all to move forward. Into the twenty-second century."

"Oh my, yes. I thought we could tee up for lunch." A panel opened in the wall and a small bar trundled out. Wright pulled a bottle of vodka from a freezer within it, dropping a few ice cubes into a glass and poured it, the ice cracking in a small fog. The lithe blond returned and placed down a silver platter of corned beef, smoked turkey, Monterey jack cheese, rye bread and cold asparagus with lemon. "You are permitted to eat and drink normally?"

He'd subsisted mostly on salty strips of hyper-nutrients provided by Dr. Rose. "I'm not that hungry. Thank you, though."

Wright slapped together a sandwich and took a big bite. He gestured for Jonathan to take the lounge chair in the middle of the room.

"So, sir - I can resume working and I'd like to."

"Of this there can be no doubt. Jonathan, I want you to look at the work that's been done in New Delhi and Johannesburg on carrier-insect infestations, while you were away."

"Yes, while I was away. I will look into that." He cleared his throat. "But my lab, my equipment…"

"Unfortunate."

"I have to… I regret whatever happened."

"At least you're all right. Learned your lesson?"

He wasn't sure what Wright, who seemed to have a confused grimace, was saying to him or how to respond. "You're right."

"You'd like us to fund you again."

47

He realized he'd been practically holding his breath and now let it out. "Yes. I'll come up with a new proposal."

"Hm," Wright said. Then in a second, "Nothing was delivered under the previous contract."

"Well... You trusted me then, I'm asking you to trust me now."

Wright's cheeks became rosier with the vodka. "I see."

"One thing I need, sir, is the back-up file of my inventory. I'm trying to re-assemble my records. Pick up where I left off."

Wright swatted his ear lobe like batting away an insect. "Yeah, Bob," he said. "Golfing buddy," he explained then turned away from Jonathan, talking softly.

He faded into himself again nervously as Wright took this call. He gave a wistful nod out the window to a lone, ruffling sail farther out on the Hudson. All of a sudden, Wright was addressing him. "See Jainchill, Jonathan. Claude Jainchill."

"Jainchill."

"He's in the main office. You know who he is?"

"Yes." He did recall the name of this corporate executive, he realized, not without a sense of satisfaction that he did, so he must have known of him early on.

"He can draw up a new contract."

"Oh. Excellent. I will - I will see him." Jonathan rose. "Good. Thank you, sir."

48

"Hold on, Bob," Wright spoke. He called out as Jonathan was exiting. "Jonathan. Don't disappoint me."

He phoned Claude Jainchill's office from the car and made an appointment for the earliest time the man could see him. Though Jonathan would have liked it sooner, he settled for Wednesday, three days away.

At dusk, he walked up the center aisle of the church in the Biosphere, passing a handful of people, half-expecting to find that Dunstan had opted out at the last minute. But a bulky envelope sat in the empty pew they'd shared that day. He snatched it up.

He drove home through mummy wrappings of fog. In the car, he pulled out of the envelope something that resembled a bobby pin, consisting of psychosensor circuits and power cells provided by Dustan. The point of the diode was to penetrate to sources of mental energies that lay blocked.

He needed external stimuli too. As far as Mitcha Ebrey, for whatever it mattered, he possessed nothing, no note, no memento at all, to prove he'd ever known this erratic, somehow frightened, somehow damaged, girl. There was no listing in public records for her address, that was the first thing he'd checked, as if she'd purposely rendered herself invisible. But he carried his notebook of class records, which he'd brought it with him to test the mind-d. He tapped the miniscule button on the tip of the unidirectional electrode like a pimple and the prod buzzed slightly in his hand. He took a breath as he fastened it underneath hair follicles. As the car drove, he thumbed through the notebook, reading names, dates, abstracts. A thistly feeling spread to the nape of his neck. But otherwise, he felt nothing physically; saw nothing in his head.

It probably should have been instantaneous, if there was something else in his class records that would have pricked recognition. He'd been foolish, vain, thinking this amateurish device would work.

At least he didn't hurt himself, he thought.

Rain slammed the roof as the car drove itself. The wipers began clacking to match the increasing force of the downpour. Even with its guidance system, the car skidded on the slick road, immersed in fog. The internal sensors flashed red - a pollution alert. He stared at the indicators.

He recognized that, of course, the car would have recorded its movements. He reset the guidance clock arbitrarily to the two months before the fire in his lab. Various sectional maps flashed before him, indicating local road trips, especially to and from the college. One map off a river road, not far from the university, also became clear. His car retained its own memory of a trip to this place - to whatever destination that was.

Soon, he rode past now-sterile farmland. Centuries-old, decaying Victorian homes were being rented out by groups of young people, from what he could observe through open blinds. Headlights burrowing through the teeming rain, his vehicle stopped automatically at its pre-programmed location.

A red door. Here. A house with no number.

He suddenly saw this in his head. The mind-d twitched and bit into him as if a sliver of barbed wire. He tore it from his scalp and shoved it into the glove compartment, shrinking from it like from a point of concentrated heat.

He remembered a red door, only that - almost nothing...

But wasn't the mind-d starting to work! Wasn't it this location that triggered the memory?

He couldn't move for a second.

Through the rain, he gazed out onto only charred acres of flattened earth. Whatever stood here had burned to the ground.

CHAPTER 10

He hid the mind-d away in the upstairs bedroom, as Diana came in. "Where'd you go?" she asked.

"I was meeting with an old student. One of the people who called me, Dunstan Booker. You never called him back."

"Oh. Was it important?"

"No." He just felt drained now by his car trip - it seemed so inconclusive as to have been futile, after all - and he didn't want to tell her what he'd been doing. He didn't want more lectures and warnings.

"What can I do, sweetheart?"

"Nothing. This is good, just to live all this again - us and Henry."

She smiled broadly and walked out. In a few moments, she called to him from downstairs. He found Henry and Diana standing and waiting for him - something was about to be staged.

Henry sat at his feet. "Watch, Dad."

"OK."

Diana pre-arranged this. The room burst to life with home movies. They were shopping somewhere at Christmastime. Jonathan picked up Henry as a smaller boy as he held out a pixie toy, like glowing glass wool in his palm, a living, dancing ornament. The younger Henry broke into a jig. He hadn't seen the boy that lively since he'd been home.

Another movie came on. The camera panned a misty shoreline and gray sea and a two-story house with a widow's walk, maybe five years earlier. This had been their house on Long Island. The rising sun glistened on dewy patches of reeds that danced in the sand. He came out the front door with a younger Diana, sexy in her bikini covered by a see-through mini-dress. He wore sandals, khaki shorts and a fisherman's cap, pushing the little boy with his fleshy grin in a stroller.

- Today is Henry's birthday - Diana said.

In the movie, Diana smiled at Jonathan in a relaxed, loving way she hadn't done since he'd been out of the clinic - like a lover from a more gentle time, or a sister he never had, the mother he'd lost.

The couple in the movie, their younger selves, advanced towards the camera. That other-Jonathan smiled too, as Diana looked into his eyes. She cocked her head and leaned on his shoulder.

- What do you want to be when you grow up, Henry?- Jonathan.

- A salesman.

That-Jonathan and that-Diana snickered and looked at each other. Henry obviously had just heard the word and didn't know what it was.

- So you will be – that-Jonathan said – you're going to be a salesman.

In the living room, he turned off the movie. That was what they had been. That was what was here for him to reclaim, he thought, and that was what she was showing him. That he didn't need to be charging around foolishly. He couldn't help it, he cried real tears - every part of his body worked - in an eruption of emotions that had felt choked in his chest. "Sorry, guys. That was great. Thank you."

Diana put her arm around him. "See? Everything's all right."

She nuzzled him, sitting on the arm of his chair. With this, Henry hugged his leg. They seemed one entity that had become malformed now re-formed. The next day, in bed alone, he watched the TV news and scenes of roadways turned into rivers and shots of the Hudson getting pelted with rain, looking like an oily beast roiling in its hushed digestion.

He got a call from Dunstan Booker. "Yo."

"How you doing, Dunstan?"

"Ain't gonna die ain't askin' why." His former student sounded drunk, as his transparent image played across the bedroom wall. "Homed in on what I gave you. I can give you a boost from the lab. Seems like the little guy is down for the count."

"The mind-d hurt like hell. I had to take it off."

"Yeah, the first time you wear it, might sting a little - it's adjusting to your brain patterns, what do you think?"

"I don't think it's any use. Wouldn't be long before my doctor's after me anyhow. I just want to go back to work. Be with my family."

"I thought you became your own laboratory."

"I tried."

"I was thinking about it, everything you said - maybe you're not as cracked as I thought in what you did. All we got is our own minds, when you think about it. The smart have gotten smarter and the dumb have gotten dumber, so aren't we the

54

smart people?... Suit yourself. One time, no charge."

The electrode hidden inside his car compelled him, like a budding addiction. In the garage, he switched on the mind-d, tucking it into the hair behind his ear, firm against his scalp.

He wore it as the day passed, slowly and uneventfully.

No memories. Now, it was a hangover of failure.

That night, Diana climbed into bed next to him. He looked into her pale blue, watery eyes, as her reddish hair tumbled past her shoulders and skirted his cheek. She tugged it away from her face. This innocent gesture made him flinch.

Diana tugs at her hair on a summer day as he stands in the doorway of their bedroom staring at her and a young man, naked under the covers- a half-empty bottle of whisky on a bedside table - Diana's nipples, bumble-bee big, exposed...

"What's the matter, sweetheart?" she asked.

The mind-d was like a fang into his head. He rushed into the master bathroom, slamming the door. He caught sight of his face in the mirror, bug-eyed, a blue vein cracking the side of his forehead. "I - I'm all right," he called to her.

"Are you sure?" she called back.

"It's nothing." He unpinned the device with a shaky hand. He shed his clothes. He turned on the faucet and stepped into the shower, taking in a lungful of steamy air. Had he caught her in bed with someone? Who, when?

He re-entered the bedroom in his bathrobe, clutching the mind-d, hot in his fist, concealing it.

She was no longer in bed. He walked past Henry's room, observing his son sleeping soundly, giving something like a fetal kick under the blanket.

Downstairs, improbably, he heard a distant, melancholy church bell. He followed the sound to the rec room in the back on the ground floor. He found her standing in the center of the room. Fragments of gray light had fitted themselves into limestone blocks and candles, phallic and candy-apple red, projected about her. At some point, she'd recreated a medieval church. A syrup of light thinned into a bronze patina of a communal convent dining room visible in the back where candles sputtered anxiously.

"So?" she asked.

He said, "Never felt better."

"OK. You have to tell me if anything is wrong."

"I know.

"My project," she pronounced. "I wanted to show it to you. Henry helped me with it."

It accounted for much of the time she'd spent without him, waiting for him. It appeared to offer her comfort. That was good. She stepped out of the room and the images dimmed behind her becoming like vapor. "You scared me," she said, lightly. "Jerk."

"Sorry."

She ran her hand softly across his hairline. "Let's go upstairs."

In bed, she reached out her arms in something like a ballet gesture and embraced him. In the soft light, her blond hair held almost a halo glow. He smelled her jasmine perfume. She crawled into a z-

56

shape, one leg between his legs, her arm stretched over his shoulder. Her fingers inched up his thigh. He tensed.

"One thing at a time, I know." She giggled. "I hope you do still love me."

"I do. Of course I do. You know, it's just... I'm trying to adjust." He didn't intend it but his voice sounded so plaintive, it shifted register slightly.

"I know," she said.

He trusted neither his own past nor his jack-in-the-box mind but he trusted her now, he trusted this. In minutes, tentatively - for him as if returning to something luxuriant he'd forgotten, like a half-remembered yet enveloping symphony, sweet and sad - they made love.

In the morning, she set out milk and orange juice on the kitchen table as Henry bounded in dressed in a red sweater for school. Jonathan watched his son eat cereal while Diana's gaze focused elsewhere, at a point in space that might have been her own patch of the past. She snapped out of the reverie and smiled at him, like a complicit smile.

Henry said, "Daddy, when you're here, everything's the best."

He squeezed Henry's hand. "You know it."

When she took Henry to school, he drove back to the college to access the library. He would keep using the mind-d but wanted to know more about possible side effects. From the car, he gazed out onto a wrecked landscape, victimized by this recent rain that had gained force until whole towns drowned in unnatural swamps. So the swollen river could give up secrets.

The screen on the dashboard flickered to life. He'd entered the names from his entire student roster and all his faculty associations as a matter of course on his very first outing to scour channels continuously for news.

Nothing turned up until today. January 15.

A newscaster's face shimmered on the screen. "Today, the remains of a female body washed ashore on the banks of the Hudson River. This has been identified as that of Mitcha Ebrey, 28, one-time postgraduate student at the State University at Kingston..."

CHAPTER 11

Mitcha's picture flashed on the screen in the car: hazel eyes, single-braided hair a kite's tail between her breasts. In the photo, she wore purple lipstick.

This was the face from his memory.

His hand quivered as the car drove to nowhere. He had to pull over for a moment to catch his breath. He forced himself to replay the news report.

Her DNA identified her though no useable DNA was discovered among her skeletal remains to point to her killer, he heard. Her body had been gutted, so when putrefaction set in releasing gases that would have made it rise in the river, instead it became fodder for omnivores. The corpse was not intended to surface: no one would know what happened to Mitcha Ebrey. It was last night's flooding that made the skull shake loose from the body's severe if makeshift moorings of everyday rope, rocks and wire, and wash ashore. Two children happened upon it. Police found the rest.

Mitcha's eyes stared at him from the dashboard screen. They blinked. He jumped. They couldn't have, it was a still photo, it was a trick of the light. A car slowed passing his, which was parked on the shoulder, probably to see if he was all right. He waved it past.

He tapped back into the news stream. Authorities had inventoried her meager possessions. Her purchases did not seem unusual or revelatory but they stopped in early February of last year,

2083. So the conclusion was that she was killed at that time.

A woman spoke onscreen, with a gaunt, sunken face that belied her corpulence, with graying hair in a monk's cut and looking stuffed into a tight brown suit. Detective Janice Cape of Homicide. Mitcha Ebrey's parents were dead. It seemed she had no living relatives. If there were any suspects in this murder, the police didn't say. Instead, Janice Cape intoned, "There won't be any more information released. This is a Canton enforcement matter."

He learned the victim's house had burned down.

He called up a related news story about this house fire. He was able to confirm that the house at the location he visited on the river road - that unlisted address - did belong to Mitcha Ebrey.

This other crime remained an unsolved arson fire. At the scene, there was also a dearth of evidence. But traces were found of Kerosote.

He'd ordered Kerosote for himself. His request hadn't been fulfilled by his college, he just discovered that.

He tried to stitch together in his head what seemed some new, confusing but critical timeline. He'd learned from the old woman Koblensk in the Climatology Lab that Mitcha dropped out of the program at their university in mid-December of 2082. After that, she lived alone, hadn't held a job and was no longer taking classes. Mitcha's activities in the ensuing days remained mysterious until her murder about seven weeks after she left the college.

The explosion and fire in his home lab occurred February 5, 2083.

The fire at her house was also reported on February 5, 2083 - precise time also unspecified, unknowable, since there were no witnesses to when and how exactly it caught fire. The same day as his lab fire.

The mind-d's power would wane. He decided he had to make use of it now. Didn't he have to? Once more, he made the car direct him back to the river road. He told himself that he would make this one last visit to the site where her home had stood, to see if he could remember anything else. Henry would be home from school before long and Diana would tend to him. As far as she knew, he was working in the college library. She was pleased about his visit to Jared Wright and knew he wanted to prepare for a meeting with his subordinate Claude Jainchill to institute a new contract. Diana counted on his re-establishing his career and reputation.

The rain had stopped. The ruins of Mitcha's house sat in an acrid black pond. He stepped out onto the wet asphalt road under an arctic-looking sky. The nearest other house, he saw beyond a grove of dead saplings, sat over two hundred yards away. At a low-income housing development next to Mitcha's place, construction had long since stalled and been abandoned, acres enwrapped by a rusted barbed-wire fence. On the other side of her house stretched someone's untilled farmland. There was no one to see who might have come and gone to her place.

No memories returned to him here. He felt dismayed and appeased at the same time. Maybe there were no memories, period. And at least, there seemed to be no provable intimate connection between this murdered student and himself. That was all that was important at this point.

He turned around to go. He found Detective Janice Cape of the Kingston police department staring at him.

CHAPTER 12

Wearing a sheer thermal rain slick and wide-brimmed brown hat, Cape appeared even more haggard in person; standing in front of her single-person vehicle, its steel-gray paint puckered, looking barnacle-ridden, with the worn insignia of the Sheriff's Department on tail fins. She was also bigger than she appeared onscreen, he saw as she drew closer, taller than he was. She gauged the expression on his face. "You know who I am."

He said, "I heard the news. So yes, I do."

"What are you doing here, Professor Kelton?"

He was rendered speechless momentarily. "Oh, of course, you traced my car."

"So what are you doing here?"

"Look, I just found out what happened. Where she lived. Just wanted to see for myself."

"Why?"

"It's horrible. I don't know... I've been in the hospital. Laid-up for a long time."

Cape said, "No personal records, no nothin'. Even her little two-year old electric tri-moto, how she commuted to the college, she kept that inside, everything up in smoke."

"No DNA," he muttered.

"Right you are. Kerosote happens to be a DNA-buster. How about that? You ordered Kerosote."

"I, no - well, yes, that's on the record. But - but you know I never wound up with Kerosote. You checked, so you know that."

63

"Your lab blew up because of Kerosote."

"What?" He felt unbalanced and leaned against his car. Could Cape possibly know this, if Dr. Rose didn't? If Dunstan didn't? There were no records made available of his fire to anyone, Dr. Rose had seen to that. But he didn't want to say that he still had no idea how his own lab blew up. All he said was, "You don't know that."

"At the time, there didn't really seem to be any connection between those two fires, yours and hers. But now there is one."

"No, there isn't." It appeared that Cape couldn't take him into custody or she would do it on the spot. So she didn't know anything further, he assumed. She was just trying to get him to tell her something. She stank of sweat herself, overheated, grasping, he thought. "You know she was my student over a year ago. That's it."

"Uh huh. Well, then, maybe you know if she had enemies. On or off campus."

"No, I don't know anything... Who reported her missing? That person will tell you."

"No one reported her missing."

He found this hard to believe. Even desperately sad. "Well, what about what about the body? You didn't learn anything significant? How's that possible?"

"The question of the body. Yes. She was stabbed to death. But somebody wanted to cover their tracks by burning down her house. Why not burn her body with it? Why move it to the river?"

Mitcha's face blazed in his head. He shifted on both feet, forcing himself to be aware of the concrete reality, dread edging in again, a sickening swell. "What are you saying, those were two separate acts? Committed by two different people?"

"Seems that way, doesn't it? What do you think?"

"No idea. As far as I know, she was killed by a complete stranger, no rational motive. You're looking at that, I assume, if there's a pattern to connect to other crimes."

"There are no serial killers anymore. You can't go twice when we know you've been there once. Or maybe you didn't hear that everybody's DNA is on file. Or maybe you take me for stupid."

His lip twitched. "I didn't know her, all right?"

"After God-zero, some folks said crime is a medical problem, Dr. Kelton. But there are things that only cops can deal with. Do you think there's such a thing as evil?"

He looked around at the sodden ground, avoiding Cape's stare. She wouldn't stop goading him and he wanted to go. "I don't know."

"You enjoyed coming to this house."

"I never came here!" He blurted this out, realizing he had come here, since his car had been able to lead him here.

Cape swiveled on one leg and spoke to her own car. "Show the man the house."

A slat opened in the roof of her narrow police vehicle and a thundercloud of light rolled out onto the black loam, building itself into a five foot scale model of a house, rising up with its half-gnawed Victorian gingerbread and buck-toothed shingles under an oppressive dun sky; weeds in the backyard looking blown flat, an antique metal clothesline on a pole rusted into its metal base at a deranged tilt.

There was a bright red front door, cardinal red. He turned away from the floating image.

"Look at it," Cape ordered.

He made himself turn around.

"Looks familiar, right? Homey."

"Look, I'll help you if I can. All right? I will."

A low, rank wind gathered force out of the putrid mulch. The fake house stood there. A blood-red door with no number...

Then he saw it with his eyes shut. It looked cleaner, a bluish tint to the worn, white shingles. It wasn't Cape's projected image, it was his own memory.

Pain shot through his head. His knees buckled and he dropped to the ground. His hand involuntarily flew to his breast pocket, where they mind-d lay hidden. Christ, he thought to himself, the device, newly infused with power - if still irregular, unprogrammable - was working by ordinary remote; as it was supposed to, it was tapping into an energy stream generated by his brain.

Cape put a hand on his shoulder. He mumbled, "I'm all right."

"Then go home to your wife and son." Cape backed away, observing him coolly as he staggered to his feet, bathed in sweat. She said, "I think you're a liar. I think you knew her well. Then you turned on her. By the way, there's no way in hell Dr. Oskar Rose can help you."

She walked off.

Back in his own car, he felt as if his head shattered like glass...

He makes his way up rickety steps to the bright red door with no number. He knocks. She opens it wearing only a sheer gown, her areolas wine-colored under the fabric, which is tied with a velvet sash. What are you doing here? she asks.

He looks past her and wonders if someone is here with her. Her mouth twists down subtly, she's not happy he's here, he thinks. He says, What's the matter, what's wrong? It's just, I had time.

How about a little later?

Later when?

So, wife busy?

Point taken, he says.

What's she doing now?

I don't know... She knows nothing about us. Even if she did –

What?

She wouldn't care, he says. She's done this too. We both do it.

Both do it, Mitcha Ebrey repeats. Oh. Good.

He hears noise from within, he thinks. But she ignores it. He says, Who's inside?

All the guys from your chemistry class.

Well, I hope they learned something.

All right, what the hell, come in, she says. She holds the door open.

He steps through the red door into the mildewed hallway. She saunters ahead as he passes through the vestibule with a sole framed Chinese print with the inscription "Deer Among Red-Leafed Maples." In it, perfect, pale brown animals stand in a grove of squat, diaphanous, scarlet trees. The animals all look in exactly the same direction. It hangs on an unpainted and peeling wall the color of

67

dirty soap. A would-be artist herself, she has said to him that Chinese painting hardly changed at all in a thousand years, they used different grades of ink, depending on how much water was added. They had shades of black.

He advances as he has several times before across the unlevel wooden floor into a shadowy interior, where the too-big and mostly empty dining room and living room with their tattered Oriental throw rugs intersect with the kitchen, with its hundred-year-old appliances.

Bottle of white in the fridge, she says.

So not only is there no one else here but she's been expecting him, he assumes. He feels buoyant, as he ultimately does around her. He throws open the refrigerator door to pull out an uncorked bottle of cheap New York State wine. Next to it lie what look like Petri dishes, which are drug compounds, along with cartridges like bullets filled with fluid. These he's never seen. They disturb him.

Suddenly, she's beside him. She says, I dreamt of having you inside me last night.

They kiss.

At some point, they drink the wine laced with a citrus-y substance from her refrigerator that turns the room pleasantly fuzzy and glowing. Time and space become a soup of broken signals. In this pleasurable swirl, they make love. In a creaking bed, she shifts on top of him with guttural moans.

In a few minutes, he finds himself lying back and staring at the ceiling of her bedroom with its cobweb shapes of splintered plaster. The atmosphere seems humid as a hothouse. A droplet of sweat runs the length of his forehead, the piquant scent of their naked bodies interlaced. He lifts himself from bed and carries a hairbrush out of the bathroom. He runs it through her hair softly, continuously as she sleeps. Slowly, she rouses. Hi, she murmurs, relishing the brush strokes. I forgot where I was.

He runs a finger gently up her arm, over fresh inch-long scars. She has cut herself - after she didn't hear from him for a week. That's what she has told him.

It seems to him there are mice scurrying somewhere. Now, like they're scratching on the walls of his skull. He needs to go home. What is Diana doing now, he wonders? He still hears strange sounds but Mitcha doesn't, she says.

The door to an upstairs room always remains closed. Someone must be up there, he thinks...

The heat grew within him, casting him into the world. He stifled a scream, jaw clenching.

Scars. What Dunstan had seen.

He sat in his car in front of the swampy flatland where Mitcha Ebrey's house had stood. Detective Janice Cape's vehicle was gone.

The other part of that discordant memory struck him. There was a room upstairs and someone who listened.

CHAPTER 13

He lurched into his house, calling out to Diana.

No response. Probably, Henry was still at school. He didn't know his own son's schedule, he thought miserably. A cloudy, floor to ceiling bubble grew in the living room. Though he knew it couldn't be so, Diana appeared to step out from it. She wore a white bathrobe.

"What's going on?" he said, his head swimming.

Her fingers joined then opened like flower petals. Standing in front of him, his wife herself seemed some wellspring of shifting realities. "What's wrong?" she said.

The rictus of pearly light around her, speckled with red candles, told him that it was some extension of her Gothic cathedral, projected here. It vanished. Words tumbled out. "I was driving, something I heard... A student I had - she was... she's dead."

Her fingers re-entwined in a prayer-like gesture. She didn't say anything.

"Mitcha Ebrey. That was her name."

"Why are you so upset?"

"I don't know, did I - I ever mention her? Talk about her?"

"Jon. Tell me. What's so important?"

"I..." He couldn't find any proper words, grabbing at them in his head. He took a deep breath and gazed out the window. Detective Janice Cape

70

was not coming for him. Their street sat forlorn as an unmarked grave.

He felt a pinprick in his neck then a rippling down his spinal cord. He turned to find Diana holding a syringe. He teetered. He collapsed into the living room armchair. He watched her replace the syringe in a jewel boxlike case that contained several glistening, small bottles and caught the glint of a screen casting variegated light. She held a drink. He wondered if she should be mixing anything with Eufonia.

"That box..." He tried to see inside it but couldn't as she closed it.

She said, "I got this from Dr. Rose. Your meds. I just gave you something that, um, helps the neuroplastic organs meld with your own tissue. That's how I understand it. Sorry it's so hands-on physical. Anyway, you need to calm down... You better come on."

She led him upstairs to bed.

A wide feather opened in his belly, a tickling calm, from whatever she'd injected him with, a narcotic effect. In this benumbed state, he thought of the whole encounter with Cape - unreal; just a rag of terror slapping him in some sudden waking nightmare.

No.

"Feeling any better?" she asked. He didn't answer. She kissed his forehead and smoothed back his sweaty hair. She said, "See, what'd I tell you? The doctor told you not to watch the news."

"Diana," he began, "Was it both of us in the old days?"

"What do you mean?"

71

"I remember… one time. You were in bed with him. Someone…"

She drew back. She giggled nervously. "Jon. What the -?... Why on earth would you bring that up now?"

"Can you tell me… when it happened?"

She fluffed her curly hair, flustered. "Well… I don't know, why?"

"You can tell me. I need to know. Please…"

"Maybe - two years ago. All right?"

So it seemed he'd lost more time from his memory than he even realized. Maybe the whole year before the fire.

Letting out a breath, she said, "I never saw him again. After that… Jon, for heaven's sake, we went through all this a long time ago. Went through it and finished with it."

"I'm sure we did - but I just don't…" He didn't want to keep pounding her with the fact that he couldn't remember. "Who was he?"

"Who?... Not that it matters. Roger."

Roger Overwater - a twenty-five year old teaching assistant at the State University. Jonathan found him in the arms of his wife. Had he stayed away from home for another hour, he wouldn't have seen any of it. So she told him.

"I don't even know where he is now," she said. "It didn't mean anything. As they say. In this case, it's lamentably true."

"All right," he said. "Thank you for telling me."

"Whew. Jon. You're throwing me… What about - what about you and this girl?"

72

"This girl... Can you tell me anything? Is there something you want to tell me?"

"Jesus, Jon. What? Did I ever meet her?"

If she hadn't seen the news, she wouldn't even know what Mitcha looked like, he realized. He didn't think he could have done something so reckless and insensitive as allowing them to meet, unless it had happened accidentally. He barely had the emotional strength but called out, "Mitcha Ebrey's picture."

The photo he'd obsessed over in the car hit the wall screen for a few seconds.

Diana stared at it. "I don't know who that is," she said. "I'm... sorry."

He heard the hurt in her voice. She guessed he was indicating an affair. She said, "Jon... I don't need to know. OK?... We don't have to do this."

"OK."

She sat back and drank some more, keeping what must have been troubling new thoughts to herself. In the silence, he wondered if, in the absence of meaningful communication between the two of them, after their move from Long Island - no doubt unhappy for Diana - they'd allowed themselves to get distracted by younger bodies and new perspectives. Maybe, simply, she cheated on him so he cheated on her. Both of theirs seemed undisciplined and callous acts.

But that was all over.

She sat with him in a bedside vigil with her whiskey. He couldn't prevent drifting into sleep, with involuntary, jerky movements, while drizzle slashed at the windows, small lines like a straight razor in the hands of a child.

He opened his eyes and Diana wasn't in the room anymore.

Lying in bed, he reaffirmed that he held pictures in his head of his own boyhood home on Long Island, a modest brick two-story with a pond in the back and a Japanese garden. He sat there and read as a boy, in dappled sunlight. He could think back to his and Diana's wedding too. It was outside on an aromatic spring day after a warm rain, under a flapping canopy, his own dad in a gray tux, his mom in yellow taffeta. And Diana - radiant, in traditional white. He thought she was the most beautiful woman he'd ever met, then, or at least the most lovely he'd dated. Ethereal in her way. Like a pre-Raphaelite painting.

That was eight years earlier. He couldn't say why it was that he and Diana had become so insular. Even at the wedding, there were few friends. He'd been a solitary boy and was a solitary man.

Anyway, he could recall those things from the more distant past. There was roughly a whole missing year in his own mind - the year before the explosion in his home lab. It was the year that Diana had a tryst with Roger Overwater. That was the year that Jonathan had an affair of whatever kind with Mitcha Ebrey.

In the opposite of what he planned earlier, now the mind-d was all about Mitcha. He called out all he could think of. "Give me any information available about Mitcha Ebrey, student at the State University of Kingston."

What appeared first on his bedroom wall screen was something that he would not have expected and startling. It was a still photo of class lab unit taken

74

for the college zine, four students sitting at a round table. One student, with uncombed, shaggy hair, hands in his lap, looked particularly dour and intense.

It was the cryptic young man who would become a terrorist. James Martinson. Sitting right next to him, smiling coyly, was Mitcha.

Anyone at the college who had a connection to Martinson would have been vetted. However, one student would not have been able to be located. Mitcha was already dead, though no one knew that at the time.

In those unaccounted-for weeks of hers leading up to her murder, she'd known James Martinson.

And Martinson set off God-zero a few months after she was killed.

For Christ's sake, he thought, was that why there was so little information being provided about her murder investigation? No wonder Cape was in a hurry to get a conviction - to protect her turf, wrap this up herself and get the credit.

What if Mitcha had discovered something about Martinson's plans and he took action against her?

Or what if there was another conspirator - who might be still out there - who'd realized what Mitcha knew - who was planning something even worse, now...

Cape implied that her murder and the arson fire at her house could have been done by two different people - two distinct events with separate m.o.'s.

Or, he thought, was he just making himself crazy?

He listened for Diana or Henry, missing the sounds of them. But he could hear nothing from the rest of the house.

A patter arose. He assumed it was the rain again, as it built to some locust-like crash against the windows. But this seemed to be inside his own head. Droplets were like human syllables - how could that be? - clustering within a big gray shell...

It sits as large as an airplane hangar, home to dozens of rows of cubicles. Some have old-fashioned curtains pulled closed on jangly rings, some under an opaque bubble of radiation; with the pinging or silent, somber light shows of medical equipment throughout the night. The university has recently opened a hospice here. It's fall. He's one of the faculty members who have volunteered at the start of this semester.

When he first sees her, she's praying. Wandering down one aisle, he's struck by the sight of this pale, svelte, young woman, with a sleek neck, graceful arms outstretched. She's a student volunteer, kneeling at the bedside of someone old enough to be her grandfather. Her black hair is braided into a ponytail. She wears purple lipstick.

The wrinkled, old man, hair a dyed tea-rose from a previous fashion trend, moves his lips quietly. The young woman bows her head then rises from her kneeling position. Jonathan affirms to himself how pretty she is - even ostentatiously so, in the sense of being out of place here, with angular features, expressive eyes he sees as somehow melancholy, perfect white skin, ineffably sensuous curves; a languid nymph. He gauges his own reaction, embarrassed - he realizes he's been standing there staring, captivated.

The breath-taking tableau comes apart. The old man shuts his eyes as she rests her hand gently on his forehead. Then she pulls the covers tighter around him, tucking him in. She sees Jonathan and recognizes that he's been staring at her. He says nothing.

He was praying, she says.

I see, Jonathan says.

A slow, steady beeping commences. He hears someone come running over. The girl looks down at her charge, who is dead.

She says, I'm Mitcha.

CHAPTER 14

That memory flitted inside him -

Since coming home from the Bluestone Clinic, he hadn't dreamed. When he awoke, it was like coming out of anesthesia. But this was something almost like his first recollection of Mitcha, when he arrived home - like a memory shattering half-sleep. He'd wanted to lay out a series of memory triggers and managed to do it by studying her college bio. Maybe what Diana gave him calmed him; somehow, it opened up channels for the mind-d to work more effectively.

So that was how he first met her. It was fall, the beginning of a new semester - it had to be in 2082. He'd gone back in his mind to the beginning.

The rain had stopped leaving behind a mulberry sky. He called Dunstan. The young man appeared to him running on a treadmill at home. Jonathan said, "Listen, you did great. You gave the mind-d a power boost and I'm starting to remember more."

"So you don't need my help no more."

"Dunstan, you have access to equipment that I don't right now. Give me another boost, OK?"

"Listen… why'd you ask me about Mitcha Ebrey?"

"I - I knew her from class and I was concerned no one heard from her, including me."

"The police talked to me."

"So what'd you tell them?"

"She was into some kind of edgeplay, I don't know what. Now she's sashimi. From what I can tell, seems like nobody knew her. The only one who ever asked about her was you, Professor."

"Dunstan, probably people would've seen us together. But that's all... You must've known that she knew James Martinson."

"Well, so what, a lot of people crossed paths with that animal."

"All I'm saying is..." He had to articulate again what it was that he did think. "Nobody seems to know how well Mitcha and Martinson knew each other, how intimate they became."

"What do you want from me?" Dunstan asked.

There was a locked room and someone who listened.

His thoughts became scrambled. "I bet someone she was seeing was responsible for her death." Someone besides him, was what he wanted to say. "You think it might even have been Martinson?"

"He's dead and so is she and I don't care."

"Wait a minute, listen, I know everything about Martinson would've been looked at. But what if there was someone else involved with Martinson, a second plotter, who figured out what Martinson told her -"

"Look, see your face in a better place," Dunstan said and hung up. He blocked his number so Jonathan couldn't call him again.

Then his lower brain hummed - some gravitational vibrato that seemed to slap at him from inside - pulling him into some other space -

They stand in an annex off the Climatology Lab. She wants to show him what she calls her magic box. In a five foot cube hangs a rotating scale model of Earth, correct in every detail from topography to potential weather patterns to the angle of rotation on the axis and the approximation of the sun's rays from artificial light.

These are conversations he doesn't have with Diana.

Mitcha wants him to witness the melting of the polar caps. Like flowing pus, ice bursts forth. The skin of the Earth gets pulled to its wide belly. The North American continent gets covered by a great new ocean. A new archipelago of mountain peaks gets left in the wake of a gelatinous deluge.

Conversely, in this world according to Mitcha the ice caps spread as frozen waste, forming land bridges over continents, as the planet turns sub-arctic - these bridges metastasizing into bulging peninsulas and finally, in a sticky cohering, into a single new continent. Nothing but a blank terrain of ice.

This is what she looks at every day; thinks about.

Either scenario, fire or ice, could result from a mega-greenhouse effect, or on the other hand, atmospheric leakage and ozone depletion; or by only a fractional shift in the Earth's axis, either by explosions from underground or impact from space.

She says, Let's say the whole of life is One Thing. Which it is - interconnected, what plant life exhales, animal life inhales, what we excrete, all the matter we leave behind, everything dead, forms new life. A cycle - , self-generating, self-perpetuating. But let's say you could introduce a viral worm directly into DNA. Which could spread instantaneously. At first, the subject unit might be one particular herd or specific eco-system. On the simplest level, sending a shock wave through a specific DNA chain, it could induce massive disruption, complete extinction, if that's what you wanted. Or else, if it's more carefully calibrated, mutations. Turn parakeets the size of eagles. Give 'em talons the size of steak knives and make them carnivores.

Of course, he says. Or render the mosquito population sterile and non-poisonous. Get locust to mutate so the species devours itself.

There you go. On the positive side, there's my gift to you for your own work. But what could be worse than a viral worm?

I get you, he says. Hypothesized.

That only means it hasn't been realized yet.

He says, A 'hypersnake'?

She nods her head and says, Total spontaneous mutation on a molecular level. Let's say Little Joey comes out on his parents' dock in Nantucket, carrying something nasty in his sippy cup. He pours it into the water.

On the revolving model of Earth, the north-eastern corner of the United States starts frothing. Then, a kind of gagging. The seas draw back from the land, receding slowly to expose skeletal rifts and hidden valleys like a mummified face. The waters re-ignite as a viscous substance that spreads, an ooze that actually spins itself into gossamer strands, wispy, white dust, wafting out into a suffocating tundra.

The oceans turn to sand.

They stand gazing not at Earth but something more like Mars. A dry, dead world.

81

That literally could happen in a matter of minutes, she says softly.

Theoretically, he says.

She says, A way to transform a big chunk of matter in the blink of an eye. Every once in a while, you get a whisper on campus about some 'hypersnake' project.

Just theory so far.

Maybe, she says. But there are things happening out there people don't know about. They're trying for extreme new things.

What are you thinking of?

She doesn't answer. He wonders if she's heard about some secret project.

She rests her hand on the lab counter, palm open - a subtle invitation. He puts his hand in hers and they interlace fingers.

Through this, they keep holding hands - it's the first time - but don't look at each other. They look at the hanging globe in front of them, yellow and cold, like the open, dead eye of one's most beloved...

CHAPTER 15

"Jonathan" - his name being called by Diana. He reached inside for his voice but couldn't find it. She appeared at the bedroom door, drying her hands on a soiled towel since she'd been cooking. "How you feeling?"

That last memory hung in his head, no, inhabited his body in the way only a dream can moments after waking.

It was the force of his own will, his own buried desire, driving these particular memories to the surface like with dreams. Maybe these memories once haunted his waking hours and so still had potent force.

Mitcha alluded to possible secret studies on campus. She could have been talking about Martinson. Yet she'd said they: "They're trying for extreme new things…"

He must have been making noises that Diana heard. "I'm OK," he managed to get out. The mind-d remained hidden from her sight. She looked at him for a long moment sympathetically, he thought, before she closed the door.

Nothing could stop the newly energized device from working - not Dr. Rose, not Diana, not he himself as long as it had power - there was no way to turn it off. When he lay back, vertigo took hold. He seemed to be sucked into it again, as though physically drawn from his bedroom into some breezy dimness. He shut his eyes and once more saw her face -

- she's pulled her hair back this time, further accentuating her long, elegant neck. He takes a seat across from her in this pub near the college, after they have visited the Climatology Lab. She orders a vodka on the rocks.

He has already mentioned Diana and Henry, his family. He has lied about nothing, he tells himself this.

Diana wouldn't be expecting him, not yet, probably another hour. He's thought about Henry, who's been failing at school. Recriminations he wouldn't mention to Mitcha, between him and Diana; making the rooms airless in his own house, with nowhere to go; what they might have done wrong, done better, who was at fault. It was some ill-seeming, tacit commonality between them that never went away. Why was Henry having trouble in both English and math? So maybe the move from Long Island was not the right idea, after all. He knew Diana had become frustrated here, unable to find a satisfying job, as he'd done. His own work remained somewhat obscure to Diana, or more probably, uninteresting - and that work was the only reason they'd moved.

He shows Mitcha pictures of his son. Her face softens.

Diana and Henry are great, is all he says.

She tells him, I would want my kid to be natural like yours. Flaws and all. Have a child in the traditional way, in a traditional relationship.

He motions to the waitress for another beer. He says, You have a partner in the venture?

Maybe.

84

He feels a gunshot of jealousy, unexpectedly. He says, You got men lined up, I know.

No... I don't know what I feel.

What do you mean?

How do people reconnect with their feelings these days? she asks.

He doesn't know what she's getting at with this disjointed conversation. He says, You tell me.

Maybe there are ways.

Seriously. Who's the lucky guy?

Is he lucky? To be with me?

I would say... yes. Anyone would be.

She actually blushes and turns her eyes downward.

He debates what to say - then stops debating with himself. He notices the booth smells sweetly of coffee and oranges, which seems sensual and inviting. His life is full of the same sterile smell, too-sharp corners, stifling, too-close angles. He feels freedom with her. In this moment, there's somehow a musical lack of corners. He says, Because you're lovely. You're beautiful, you don't need me to tell you that. And your work is brilliant. You're dedicated to it and it's important. What we both do - you and I - it's what has to be done. It means the future

A moment passes. She says, This is nice here. Us, like this.

He's surprised, delighted. He watches her, she doesn't look up, like she's lost in a thought. Yes, it is nice, he says, I'd like to do it again.

He thinks that it's a bland statement but full of expectations, like a blank piece of paper he's handing to her.

85

But she doesn't respond and keeps looking down. He casts an eye across the dimly lit pub. Two men sit at the bar. He takes them for Canton police, plainclothes, thinks he recognizes them from their patrols on campus by-ways. One downs shots of whisky. Through the tinted windows, the night outside looks phosphorescent. Inside, you could become giddy just with the heavily oxygenated air. Music plays softly, a non-descript, synthetic jazz instrumental, riffs and chords on a loop, a mechanical swirl, riding the air like the tangy odors.

Mitcha sips her drink, chews on the ice. She tells him, What you say, things you say, it's because you don't really know.

The two cops at the bar happen to glance at them, he notices.

He leans in, drawn into her glistening green eyes. He wants to take her face in his hands like a child. He asks, What don't I know?

She says, You don't know me -

He bunched his bed sheets in his fists, fighting off co-mingling realities, trying to tamp this new one down. The mind-d had achieved astonishing power, setting off some catalytic reaction. Almost like vomiting.

Even with the queasiness, he craved being with her again, and in spite of knowing it was wrong. This feeling rose in him like a tide engulfing the room, which itself seemed to swim into pointillist phantasms behind his eyes as he shut them and lay still: he got re-folded into another time and place once more as he felt himself lying on damp grass and he heard her voice again -

New Zealand, that's the place, she says.

86

New Zealand, he says. Why?

She says, The Druse colony says it's fully functional and self-sufficient. They found a corner of New Zealand. And they can start again, live like human beings. Adam and Eve in the Garden of Eden.

Mm. But you know, agrarian communes have a long history. They pretty much devolve into cults, even the best-intentioned ones - become so inbred and isolated, or corrupt, they wither.

Thank you, my guru.

Well, am I wrong? he says.

They're lying in her backyard, which looks out on an open field. He thinks she's simply telling him that she wants to run away, which pains him. He says, I'm telling you, we're fighting the good fight here.

I'm not sure what I'm fighting for anymore, she says.

He thinks sometimes that their conversation means nothing yet at the same time, it's the only thing in his life that means anything.

He tells her, You have your life in front of you.

In a second, without saying anything, she clasps his hand in the same way he did hers in the Climatology Lab. This is their most personal, symbolic gesture, he thinks.

She unzips his black jeans and reaches in, stroking him. Lying on the damp earth, he watches her face, lets her do what she's doing, what they're doing for the first time...

He yells out her name, Mitcha -

In a minute, they both come together. A few seconds later, she says, I'm scared.

87

She says this with Jonathan still inside her.

A low trill sounds. She swats at a phone-pin on her unbuttoned orange shirt, breasts exposed. He grimaces at the timing, that someone would be calling her. Could it be Diana! How would that be possible? That's just his guilt trying to find a voice, he tells himself.

Who -? he blurts out in spite of himself, supporting her weight on top of him.

She relaxes on top of him, breathless.

Who was on the phone? he says again.

Who?... Zachariah.

Zachariah? Who's that?

Zachariah Willer. He, um, whatever - works the line on storm damage. On the river.

Oh... So that's the guy. That's your boyfriend.

Well. In his mind... He could be spying on us right now.

Spying on us? Jesus. Is that what you were scared of? Is that what you meant?

Yes, she says, after a moment. But she doesn't look at him and he can't tell what she's really thinking.

She rolls over onto the grass next to him.

She says, He did follow me that one time...

He followed you? he repeats.

A bloody lip opens in the sky, drooling red, lovely and eerie at the same time. She says, Aurora.

He knows it's chemical dissipation, various, high-airborne pollutants interacting with water vapor at the right temperature and altitude to bend light.

He's startled to see a tear rolling down her cheek. She brushes it away quickly.

88

What's wrong? he asks her.

Nothing, she says.

Orbits of contradictions seem to widen away from him, even as she holds him. The two of them lie on the damaged earth under the bleeding sky clinging to each other -

The memory sheared off.

Zachariah Willer. Whoever that was, that was someone she was seeing besides him. At that moment, that was whom she was afraid of.

CHAPTER 16

Diana strode back into the bedroom like an attentive nurse. She sat on the bed and placed her hand on his forehead. "You don't have a fever. But you look flushed."

He noticed she'd changed outfits for dinner. She wore a pumpkin-colored silk blouse with a low-cut, lacey collar. She carried a tiny, shimmery white box. He didn't know what that was and it irritated him, he didn't want any more surprises.

"I'm OK," he said hoarsely. His brain burned as he lay there, still though agitated. With a lull in this peristalsis of recall, he admitted, "I've been remembering things."

"Good. What things?"

"I… actually, I was thinking about the girl who was murdered."

"That!"

"Listen, Diana…" He sat up shakily, leaning on his elbow. "The police will be checking up on people who knew her, obviously. So…"

"What do you have to tell them?"

"What I'm telling you is I've been trying to - to figure out details myself. Just to be prepared." A razor sting in his head contorted his face for a second and he turned away from her. "Whatever happened between us is of no consequence, I'm sure. Still -"

She looked at him warily. "So then…" She paused. "What the police should get from you is silence."

"Yes. Exactly. That's what they'll get. Silence."

"Jon, I don't want Henry involved."

"Oh, hell no, me neither. We'll make sure of that... Has he ever - did he ever see anything, hear anything? You and I, we've both done things..."

"All he knows is that his two parents love each other. And him. That's all he ever had any reason to believe."

"Well, then, good." He wanted to get off the subject of Mitcha Ebrey too, for both their sakes. Diana didn't know about the vortex of the past into which he'd spun himself. Probably she was right and no one needed to know about it, ever. He said, "You know, I spoke to a woman at the college before who was one of the survivors too. How did you and Henry escape it?"

"Why do you want to keep going over painful things? I mean, really -"

"I don't mean it to be painful. If I know things... I feel more whole."

"Well... If you happened to be inside... if you never went out during or after - in a sealed off environment, then you had a chance."

"So where were you and Henry?"

"My project," she said. "The convent and the church. Creating the reconstruction means a kind of sterile environment, cut off from the outside. Like a hermetically enclosed black box theatre."

"I do know that," he said.

"Until it becomes free-standing, then it can be moved around. So I was in there, in the rec room. With Henry."

"That's so amazing, so lucky."

"Toiling away. It was like you in your lab for all those weeks, day and night - right up until the accident. That's why sometimes you and I barely saw each other then... Anyway, Henry and I had to stay in the house for days after it hit. And then, only go out with the facemasks. But we were OK. I knew you were recovering too. So that's how I knew..."

"Knew what?"

"That we were saved."

Probably she'd used her cathedral to pray as well. "And we are."

"That's why I brought you this." She took the top off the little, white box to reveal two gold rings on a pillow of cotton; so that was what it was. She plucked out one of them and placed it on his ring finger. Both her hands clasped his and he felt this warmth as a coursing into his limbs. "Your own wedding ring is gone."

"Yes." Smelted along with his outer flesh. "Thank you."

"This one is mine." She placed the gold wedding band back on her own finger. "I never took it off... Do you remember when you gave it to me?"

"Long Island. Montauk. Yes, I do remember - we just spent the night at a motel on the beach." He floated back effortlessly to a serene seaside in his head, without any of the tectonic shifting of the mind-d. "We drank margaritas. Danced. And we realized then -"

She finished his sentence. "That we were the only ones for each other."

"No one else could be such a good match."

92

She kissed his lips tenderly. "Till death parts us," she said.

"Till death parts us."

"These are our vows. That's all that matters now. To love each other wholly and fully, and with respect and faithfulness."

He improvised blandly. "To love each other this way from now on, always."

In a second, she said, "Sometimes things break. But you put them back together. As best as you can."

She held his hand and the doorbell sounded in predictable, pernicious juxtaposition to this moment.

Janice Cape's height and girth practically filled up the doorframe as she stood in her rain slick. A police van sat parked in the street and two men in navy blue cloaks with face helmets leaned against it watching her.

He said, "How can I help you, Detective Cape?" Diana came up behind him. Jonathan told her, "Honey, please check on Henry."

She hesitated for a second, looking Cape over then vanished into the interior of the house.

"She's an attractive woman. I don't know why you would cheat on her."

Dr. Rose's face appeared on the wall screen in the living room. Jonathan knew he was being watched from within, unbelievably and appallingly, by Rose - but then, Janice Cape probably didn't. Rose seemed to be asserting his authority over her. Cape spotted the doctor's image but said nothing.

"So what's up?" he asked. Cape wouldn't know how much he both desired and dreaded that answer.

"Dunstan Booker, your student, says you were fixated on Mitcha Ebrey."

"How could I be fixated if I barely knew her?"

"She was the first thing you asked the kid about. He figured you wanted to find out how much he knew about the two of you. He knows you and she were having an affair."

"I... don't believe he said that. That's not what he thought."

"So what were you doing when she was killed, the day of February 4th last year?"

"You can't fix the exact time she was killed. The body was - it was too decomposed."

Cape let out a laugh. "When she was pulled out of the water, a blue crab crawled out of her chest cavity. How do you like that?"

"So what difference does it make what I say?"

"February 4th. She didn't purchase anything after that day. It fits the bone analysis too."

He wondered what Cape could have pieced together about Mitcha's life. Everything about it seemed so damn flimsy. What was it she'd bought then, he thought, absently?

Cape answered the question without his asking. "Just a small bit of food, veggies and the like. But then - guess what? Nothing else, no records of her anywhere. Her house gets torched the very next day, February 5th. So the 4th is the date we're going with. That all right with you?"

"Look..." He remembered what Diana just said, that they barely saw each other in those weeks leading up to the fire, while he was spending time in the lab. "Mostly, then, I was working - all the time, in fact."

"Does anyone know that for sure, who could confirm a time frame for you?"

"Would you expect someone to remember one whole day almost a year ago? After everything we've both been through? I was working in my home lab. Alone. That explanation should be good enough for you."

"And your lab got wrecked, with all its records, so that's handy."

"Not purposeful on my part."

"Anyway, whatever happened to you happened the day after Mitcha Ebrey was sliced up."

"You must know she had a boyfriend, a guy named Zachariah Willer. She was afraid of him."

"Yeah, she had a boyfriend. All the more reason for you to become jealous," Cape said.

"That's what you think?"

"Here's what I think. Kerosote is not so easy to get. But you wanted to for your home lab, you tried. That's what lit up her house. I believe you did get it. I believe it was you who burned her house down with it. And I believe, right after you did that, it's how you set fire to your lab accidentally." She reached into her pocket and removed what looked like a silver coil. She grabbed his hand forcibly and before he could stop her, she slipped this bracelet onto his wrist, where it automatically became tight and irremovable.

"What is this?" But he knew he was under house arrest.

"Jonathan Kelton, you're a suspect in the murder of Mitcha Ebrey. You're forbidden from traveling outside a twenty mile radius of your front door."

The police could keep track of him with something smaller than a pinhead so this visible indication of a police monitor was part ostracization, further humiliation and meant as a glaring reminder to him of his predicament. Dr. Rose gazed sphinxian from the screen.

"Are you aware of what will happen if you venture outside of the twenty mile radius?"

"No," he said.

He glimpsed a smirk. "If you do, under current Canton Code, we're authorized to shoot to kill."

"But - no, wait a minute. What about her connection to James Martinson too?"

"We've always known that she knew him, so what?"

"In a group photo from the college, they're sitting next to each other, close to each other, two other students in their lab unit are positioned further away. That means something."

"That would be convenient, to blame a dead man."

"You said so yourself that there could've been two separate crimes, her murder and the fire at her house. It occurred to you that other people could've known what Martinson was up to - and it occurred to you that he might not have been working alone, no matter what the final report was. Someone else could've come after Mitcha if - if, let's say, she became a threat to their plan -"

"What do you know about it?"

"I… nothing. But look, could just one person really have kept everything secret like he did, operating within the university, getting the access he did, plus the equipment, the funds? He must've had help."

"I want you to step aside. I got a warrant to search your house and your car. That's all I'm interested in. I'm coming in."

CHAPTER 17

Rose spoke from the screen in the living room. "Detective Cape, if you set foot in the house you'll be terminated from the force."

Cape's eyes narrowed. "What the fuck are you talking about?"

"Your warrant has been superseded. Check now. You and your officers must leave the premises. You cannot enter this house. You cannot make further demands upon Dr. Kelton or his family."

"What if I want a lawyer?" Jonathan said to the doctor's image.

"The Bluestone Clinic will take care of any eventuality. No one else need ever be involved and won't be."

Cape pulled out a palm filer from her pocket and gazed at it. Whatever she saw made her eyes turn inward and the corners of her mouth droop. She looked at a loss for a moment. Jonathan stood his ground watching her. She recovered to snarl at him and at the wall screen, which went blank. She said, "You think you can hide behind new goddamn medical codes?"

"I don't think anything," Jonathan said. "You see it's not my doing."

Cape stared at him. How did she see him? That, as in history, he was Jack the Ripper unmasked as a royal physician, a scientist-butcher? Now, maybe, even, Frankenstein's monster? He held out his chained wrist to her. "Take this off?"

"No, that stands. Until further notice! He can't do anything about, I already told you, not in the end, he can't." She spat on the yellow-brown grass then spun on her heels towards the waiting van.

His heart palpitated. He looked back at the wall screen, still blank. "Dr. Rose, will you talk to me?" There was nothing. What was Rose himself thinking, at this point, about him?

Diana appeared at the top of the stairs, looking pallid and pitiable now in that carefully chosen outfit for supper. She looked at the silver bracelet and her eyes widened. She knew what it was. "Jon."

He recognized by now their Eufonia glow but was glad for it. "They don't know what they're doing, the cops."

"So what's that?"

"This is just a stupid formality."

"Jon. What'd they find out? Tell me."

"Nothing at all. Dr. Rose has complete jurisdiction anyway. He knows I've got nothing to worry about." He said in an unnecessarily louder voice to Rose, "Isn't that right?" He felt a weird giddiness knowing that someone else was inhabiting his body.

She descended the steps mincingly, wobbling. "Then... if she bothers us again, I'll talk to her. I'll make sure she stays away."

He tried to veer away from painfully untenable speculation about what Detective Janice Cape might do. "Henry hear anything?"

"I don't think so, I hope not."

He hid the bracelet he wore under his shirtsleeve and sought out his son in his bedroom.

99

Henry was sitting at his desk. Oddly, he stared into a bank of five screens that were all blank.

Jonathan said, "Hey, buddy." He sat on Henry's bed and stared at the boy concernedly but Henry didn't look at him. "What's up?"

"Just here," Henry said.

"Oh… you feel OK?"

"Yeah. Daddy, can I ask you one question?"

"Sure."

"You love me and Mom?"

"Of course I do. You never have to worry about that."

"You weren't home for such a long time."

"Henry, I was in the hospital. I had an accident. A bad one."

"I wasn't allowed to see you."

"Up to me, you would've been there every day."

"OK."

The boy turned back to his bank of blank screens. Jonathan had once thought of them as rabbit holes representing an endlessly recycled cultural past, or now, the controlled dissemination of news, current misinformation and disinformation. He said, "Maybe you'd like to watch something."

"I will," Henry said. "I know what to do. I remember."

"Henry, why would you say that?"

"No reason."

Downstairs, he asked Diana, "Is Henry taking Eufonia too?"

"Well." She looked surprised. "So you discovered that."

100

"No, but I wondered... He's acting a little strange."

"I told you, he's all right. Amazingly."

How could he challenge her? "I know you've been keeping tabs on him. Anything that helps you both cope is good."

"That's the point," she said, and went back to cooking.

Not long after, the three sat down together to eat chicken and mashed potatoes. Henry and Diana acted composed but didn't talk much. She sat straight-backed and with her shoulder-length, flaxen coif and newly rouged cheeks, she looked somehow aristocratic. Jonathan thought that he'd get used to their respective changeable behavior. The dinner seemed as if it was a rite, something formal; whatever yearnings existed finding expression in the simplest gestures of sharing at the table.

Alone, after dinner, he looked up Zachariah Willer. He proved easy to find. He was a public employee and it was an unusual name. He worked for the Hudson River Patrol. They called themselves the Hudson River Hawks. They were assigned to take water and soil samples, checking for toxicity levels, measuring an increase or decrease in river volume. For hundreds of miles, the river bottom sat below sea level, while in an unusual way, the Hudson could move in two directions at once; it was possible to see ice floes near the bank moving north while floes in the center moved south. It had sealed its place as a barometer of climatological changes. Zachariah Willer and his hastily trained team were among the river's new caretakers, since God-zero.

They also doubled as an autonomous river crime unit, under Canton law. The Hawks had the run of the river. Guns were hard to get these days but they had them. They carried an array of knives, whether for cutting anchor lines, deadwood, or dissecting deep-water fish. The largest knife they carried could have doubled as a butcher's knife, to gut or amputate.

A picture of that knife, as sharp as was humanly possible, dangled in front of him, glistening silver. He closed down the site. He got an image in his head of the knife being driven into Mitcha Ebrey over and over again.

CHAPTER 18

When he woke up with Diana the next morning, he asked her to remind him where he could find his parents. He considered that they might be sources of information too.

In his car, he spoke the name "Alba." This was within his twenty-mile radius proscribed by Cape. The vehicle steered him onto the open road. Alba was comprised of four buildings without windows, fifty stories each, oyster-gray, each aligned with a point of the compass. He parked and made his way up a flagstone walkway. His destination was a building that stood to the east, with a statue probably meant to depict a flock of birds scrambling from the ground in some long ago migratory launch - like souls ascending - but which seemed to him with its Expressionistic angles like birds flooding through a jet engine.

Inside, he rode the elevator to the tenth floor and walked in to a small room with fake knotty pine walls and a settee. "It's me, Jonathan."

Frank glimmered to life in an armchair, Katherine standing next to him in a lime-green housedress.

"You look good, Johnny," his mother said.

"Haven't see you in a while, son," said Frank.

He sat, looking at an ECO of each of them - an Electronically Created Organism, unsleeping and diligent; a free-standing, free-associating manifestation in the image of its subject. His parents had been here, in this state, for approximately six years; preserved when he and Diana lived on Long Island, then he moved them up here.

"I've been hospitalized."

"Oh, no," his mother said.

"Listen, did I ever speak about what I was working on? Working with. In my lab at home? Like Kerosote, for example?"

They couldn't answer that. They looked through him into electronic oblivion.

"OK. I visited you a lot, didn't I? Before that?" His own voice sounded hollow to him. But these limpid phantoms retained some semblance of memory as far as what he'd imparted to them in their meetings. He could very well have come here in the months prior to the explosion in the lab, while he was still seeing Mitcha. But would he have spoken to his parents about a mistress? Could he have used this as a Confessional? "Mom and Dad, did I ever mention Mitcha Ebrey?"

"That name doesn't ring a bell," Frank said.

A rush of air escaped his lips, in his frustration. "Nothing about someone named Mitcha Ebrey, you sure?" No further response. "Zachariah Willer?"

Nothing. No, that name would have been unlikely. Meantime, the mind-d, formidable as it had been during the spurt of activity earlier, was turning less effective with power draining. He would have to find another energy source. A simple electrical charge from a wall socket wouldn't do, of course, that was why Dunstan had helped him to begin with: it needed a more concentrated dose of electricity, if he could find one. But he would continue to wear it. Before Dr. Rose - strangely

104

silent about it, but for how long? - stepped in; or it just burned out for good.

This little room with no outside light became stifling. Like just an old storage closet. Self-pity overcame him, which he'd been pushing away. He had to remind himself that he was here for a reason, to question them, not for emotional comfort, of which there was none. "Did I ever do anything wrong?" he asked.

Katherine raised her hand, palm held high facing him, maybe some bizarre glitch.

"Is there something I told you that you don't want to repeat? Is that what you mean?"

Katherine said, "We don't understand you."

"Look, I'm worried as hell because I can't remember what I did during the year before I went into the hospital. Then this girl I knew intimately turns up dead…"

His father asked, "You remember when you were eight years old and we bought you that puppy, a loveable, little mutt?"

At once, he realized what they were going to remind him of. He fidgeted.

"You named it Harpo, after one of the Marx brothers."

Katherine said, "Because of its frizzy hair."

"It was terrible when we lost the dog. I remember how you cried, Johnny."

"Hit by a car," Frank recalled.

"That's right, dear. Poor Johnny inconsolable. We didn't know what to do."

"You didn't want him anymore," Katherine said. "After he bit you."

105

"He was rabid," his father said. "You just didn't know what to do."

He didn't say anything - as if sprockets, however mangled, by conscience, by time, by his present jack-in-the-box of a brain, flipped images back into view. The dog attacked him, foaming at the mouth, white spittle in a cottony ball on its jowly chin. He sprayed it with lighter fluid and threw matches at it to keep it away. The dog yelped as the fire pecked at his fur at first then took big, bright bites out of it, sending the dog into total madness, it seemed, as it burned, dashing into the street.

"Remember what I told you then, Jonathan?" Frank squinted. "The creatures of the Earth are not ours to keep. We're like caretakers, that's all. Soon, things are enfolded once more into their great and natural place."

"The point is," his mother said, "that whatever you're facing now, please don't lose sight of the natural cycle. We must remember that separation should not be cause for despair. We never meant to leave you."

"You were always a good boy," Katherine said.

He doused a dog with lighter fluid and set it on fire. He said, "I could never kill someone."

They stood speechless for a second. Then his mother said, "You look good, Johnny."

Minutes passed and he lost track of time, as his parents went silent as lamplight. This program seemed defective. For a second, he thought about deleting it, to save money. But he didn't.

The dog bolts into the street wearing a coat of flame. It gets smacked by the oncoming car and catapulted to the side of the road. Its blood oddly sparks and spreads over mineral grit on the asphalt like an oil spill. Jonathan at eight years old stares at this crushed body for a long time. He does nothing, as if bewitched...

There must have been some kind of an emotional lack, that he did not feel empathy in that moment. But he'd just been a child. Even if one with a trait that might lead an adult - in some wracked mindset - to set someone's house on fire.

CHAPTER 19

He walked out of Alba to his car in a cold wind. For now, all he could think to do was find Zachariah Willer - someone very much alive and once involved with Mitcha - to learn what he knew, in what Jonathan pictured as a race to keep up with Janice Cape. He set off for what was a public housing complex in Rhinecliff, an old, crumbling riverside town. Thunder rolled off the river wind, as he spotted two red brick pillars rising in the midst of desiccated trees offered a sign: "The Woods." It underscored a ludicrousness about the place. He drove down a dirt road, bronze statues of deer - extinct in these woods now - lining the shoulder. Stone buildings stood in a clearing with winding paths intersecting, each with hanging, wooden street signs with names like Maple Grove and Elm Terrace, belying the fact that the soil around them recently lay gasping and dying. Window boxes full of fake petunias and pansies bent in decorative crescents around the street signs, like the smiles of the insane.

He walked into the manager's office. A middle-aged black man with close-cropped, gray hair sat cross-legged on the floor, eyes closed, puffing a pink cigarette. Smoke hung in the air, an iridescent kaleidoscope.

"I'm looking for Zachariah Willer."

The man opened his eyes slowly, in his dulling wrap of drugs. "Who's you?"

"A friend. I heard that his girlfriend died. Just wanted to tell him I'm sorry."

"I don't know what you're jabberin' about."

The man's eyes rolled up in his head, giving an effect that he was blind. Jonathan squatted to eye level with him. He didn't move from his cross-legged position on a green carpet so worn it looked like a sea of algae. "Please, is this guy here or not?"

The man said, "Moved out. Ain't nothin' in his room. I sanibombed it already."

The room had been sterilized of all organic matter, he could figure what that meant. "Why'd he leave?"

"He don't converse... HRH."

"What?"

"Hudson River Hawks. That's what they call they-selves. What's written on they cars. Willer works outta Storm King."

"So where'd he go?"

The man looked directly at Jonathan. "He don't say where. And he don't say why... Few days ago."

When Mitcha's body surfaced, Zachariah fled.

Outside, Janice Cape approached him on the path. Next to her a sallow man walked at a brisk pace to keep up, so diminutive as to seem a deformity. He wore a bulky wool coat, dyed violet, hair like upturned tree roots in a tangle of dreadlocks. Jonathan could see a tiny blue triangle shape branded into the upper right side of his forehead: the man was a drug abuser, a willful outsider; in the event of another mass emergency, his caste was expendable. Cape kept her eyes trained on Jonathan from under her wide-brimmed

109

hat as she moved in, while the one next to her looked around, sizing up his surroundings with ape-like curiosity.

"So you two know each other," she said.

The little man took a second. "No. Don't know him. Never seen him."

Cape's eyes flashed annoyance. The sky growled. All three of them looked up, looking for a warning sign of anything, in this now-commonplace but still bizarre collective experience.

"Who is he?" Jonathan asked Cape.

She didn't respond but the man did. "Quinton Lent," he said.

"Ring a bell?" Cape asked.

"No bells."

Quinton Lent said, as if heavy with meaning, "We was close."

"We who?" He guessed, "You and Mitcha Ebrey?" He said to Cape, "Where'd you dig him up?"

"She hadda interrupt my polo game," the man said.

Speaking directly to Cape, Jonathan said, "Look, why are you hounding me? It was Zachariah Willer who wouldn't leave her alone. Now he's gone! You see that. He worked the river. The river was where her body was found. He'd know how to hide a body there - that's not the easiest thing in the world. Plus, the river patrol guys carry guns and knives, legally, all the time."

She tugged the dwarfish man by the coat sleeve. "Come on," she said angrily. She turned back to Jonathan. "This doesn't mean a thing," she said - referring to the fact, presumably, that this man had not i.d.'d Jonathan positively as Mitcha's lover, or in some other way. She said, "I know you wanted to find out if Willer told anybody anything, what he might've said. No innocent person would do that."

"No, that's not true, Detective. I'm..." Should he tell her he didn't remember? Did she know? Would Dunstan might have told her that? Cape started walking away. This time, he didn't want her to leave, he wanted her to tell him something. "Who the hell is this guy anyway?" he called to her.

It was Quinton Lent who responded. "Foster brother."

"Foster brother?"

"She came out of Clark," he volunteered. He was validating that he knew her at all, passing on personal information.

"Clark..." Jonathan wanted to place that but couldn't.

Quinton Lent kept looking back at him. "Yeah. What do you think of that?"

The pair vanished past a tangle of tree branches. Then he teetered where he stood, with a feeling like pincers gripping his head. The leaden sky appeared to close in. His perceptions became inverted, like he was plummeting down an invisible chute -

I want to show you the place I was born, she says, as he drives.

Love to see that, he says.

She's told him nothing about her upbringing. They sit in his Ford Roguebat, on this bleak, late fall day. They pass a sign for the town of Catskill.

Home sweet home, she says, before long.

111

She asks him to pull over. What they're looking at is an abandoned lab facility, one wall blackened by fire, the glass entry doors smashed. The edifice sits vandalized and empty. A metal sign out front reads Clark Laboratories. Someone has defaced it with sophomoric graffiti of a penis and vagina.

At first, he's bewildered, turns towards her, he doesn't get it. But then he does. He says, You were born here.

Yeah. And I have such fond memories.

The Clark Institute. She was a test tube experiment. An anonogen. Jefferson Clark, eccentric multibillionaire, purchased unclaimed, warehoused sperm and egg donor specimens. Some said he was a visionary, as he sought to assert nurture over nature, in a contained counter-revolution against bio-engineering - raising babies in a lab environment to be enriched by accelerated learning in his new behaviorist paradigm. In this special school for these orphans, kept purposely without families, he would create geniuses who would go on to glory and riches. But the experiment was inconclusive and ended abruptly. He died a broken and broke old man; his children, his bastard seeds, scattered to the wind.

Apparently, like Mitcha.

How long did you stay here? he asks her, fighting the urge to say, 'were you imprisoned here.'

Four years... Five of us in that batch. I don't really remember the others, or know where they are. How could we know what was happening? Suddenly, some nanny figure or someone you

112

thought was your relative disappeared, and the numbers of the grown-ups started to shrink. I think when the lights went out in one wing was when I got really frightened. Finally, somebody stepped in, some government agency, and we got farmed out as adoptees.

This would explain what he's starting to see as a preoccupation by her on having a natural child in a traditional way.

But the adopted family was OK. Nice people really, she says.

I'm glad. Where?

Outside Seattle. Cool place. But I went off to college on the East Coast.

They give you a lineage? he asks gently.

No.

What about your adopted family? You close?

They're mostly gone.

Sorry, he says.

He'd like to know more about her adopted family but she doesn't elaborate.

She says, It prepared me for one thing, though, I think. Coming from here.

What's that?

It's that - you can't predict anything. You have to be able to endure pain. Make room for it in your life.

I'm not sure -

I want to go in, she says.

Why?

Do you believe that one way to face your fears, your pain, is to drown yourself in them? Then you find air. You force yourself to. Then you can survive.

113

What are you afraid of?

Maybe… that I'll be left alone.

I'm here, he says.

Maybe… I'm still back in there, she says. She points to the ruined building. Maybe I never left.

What do you mean?

I mean I can never escape what I felt back then.

He touches her arm. Don't say that.

She says, I've never done this before, come here like this.

Mitcha, look at what you've become. You've got so much to give to the world. I keep telling you that.

She starts walking down the path then looks back at him. This is where the moat was, she jokes, Watch your step.

He follows her. He's resigned; more, glad she's doing this with him; that he's the only one she wants to do it with, or at least that she says that he is.

They step through the jagged glass of the smashed front door. A barren, chartreuse hallway reveals itself dimly, defaced with squiggles of graffiti, some hieroglyphs of a ruptured Id.

The hall isn't straight, he sees. It zigzags before them.

She says, It was purposely an altering of perceptions. There were signals, signs. One door that opened to one room one day another day might not open to the same room. But there were clues to let you know - you couldn't just, like, proceed. You had to be constantly diligent and looking for clues. That was all part of the teaching method. He didn't want Pavlovian responses… What a nutcase.

114

Confusing for a child, definitely, he says.

She says, Fucking nutcase... All he did was, like, blow on a dandelion, send the fronds into the air to land anywhere, a flowering of nutcases.

A window appears at the end of the twisted corridor, looking like stained glass. It offers a likeness of a man with glasses, a thick book open in his lap and with a faraway look. She says, Our fearless leader.

It's unbreakable glass, Jonathan realizes. But someone has managed to drill through both eyes.

She says, I always wondered what Clark was looking off at. Maybe the young girls taking a piss. I thought that later, to amuse myself.

He's dead, Mitcha. He can't hurt you. This is all in the past.

She takes him by the hand, leading him through a half-opened steel door into what was once a laboratory. There are big glass tanks, broken. What would Clark have kept in there? Freezer doors hang open, exhaling hot air from empty space.

Look, she says.

What?

She waves a finger at each corner of the ceiling, where a tiny camera eye pokes out. She says, Surveillance. Everywhere. The eyes of Jefferson Clark. He saw everything, watched everything. As babies, you knew nothing. You found out later. Clark was like, how could you describe it, like primitive tribes must have first thought about the gods, or God - nothing proven, speaking about it in whispers, trying to put together signs that might or might not make sense. Knowing there was something… else. Just not sure what. So you're a little afraid, and in awe.

God's eyes, he says.

Yeah. Like that.

She grabs him, saying, Let's make God proud.

In this awful room, under cobweb shapes of plaster in the ceiling, she shoves his hand into her pants. She says, There is something about… being like a child. Helpless. It has to do with how your energy's directed.

She inserts his finger into her, ferrying it in and out. She says, Harder.

She unbuttons her shirt and squeezes her own breasts, nipples stiffening. He shoves three fingers into her with force.

She slaps him.

His head reels. Then he backhands her. He grabs her wrists, pinning her against a lab table, both of them panting. He needs to quell his own ache, won't let her just taunt him this way. The air in the room feels heavy, with a bittersweet stink like autumnal rot.

Her cheekbone unzips blood. You hurt me, she says.

Sorry, I thought you -

Yeah, it's all right, she says. That's it, that's what I want.

She pulls out something that looks like a taser from her pocket -

This memory cut off like the others. He fell, yelling out, pinpricks beneath his scalp. The mind-d had reactivated with its last reserves of power and now it dropped him in a flameout within his own head.

116

She came out of Clark. What Quinton Lent said was what it took to trigger that memory.

That particular memory and whatever it might mean.

The apartment manager approached him, letting out a gravelly, deep cough. He said, "You look ready for the bone pile."

Bile rose and he vomited.

117

CHAPTER 20

He waited until Diana and Henry were asleep to look up Quinton Lent. The brand Quinton wore on his forehead meant he was registered in a national database. He found a phone number - which meant the man was traceable no matter where he was - with the notation "NFA" for No Fixed Address. He phoned a number that was also listed and surprisingly, Quinton answered right away, as though he was waiting for this call. He said little but eagerly suggested meeting at a place he picked, Bar Far.

He found Diana in bed, her mouth hanging open, one arm extended in the direction of a shriveled Eufonia patch on the floor next to a whisky tumbler. He dressed in silence. Downstairs, he tapped the refrigerator door and left a spoken message for her. "Diana, I just met a guy and I'm not sure who he is - but I - I hope he can help me fill in some blanks. That's all I'm trying to do. So don't worry. I'm going out to meet him."

Earlier, passing by the living room, he'd been startled at the sight of nuns loitering, swathed in heavy black and white cloth and with blank eyes. Diana had stood alone in a corner, her back to him. Her words seemed charged with emotion, though inaudible, murmured to a black-clad figure that hovered an inch above the floor, motionless and stone-faced. Diana was praying. He imagined that for his wife there was a deeper communion - the veiled, distant women compelling her with the authority of her own mother. She'd been abandoned at seventeen, when her mother ran off - and her dad was killed in a car accident when she was a little girl. He knew she'd gone through a promiscuous period as a teen, she was open about that when they first met. He'd had only a handful of lovers and Diana more than him. Since age 20 or so, she'd been taking medication to fight off depression. Eufonia was only the latest and probably the best.

He slipped on a light jacket and emerged into the chilly, moonless night. Before long, off Route Nine, he caught sight of two-foot letters spelling out "Bar Far" projected into an ellipse in a parking lot. There were few other cars. He walked to the unmarked wall of the one-story building that faced the lot in this industrial park. A red slit appeared like a surgical cut and he shoved in his credit card. A metal door slid open and he stepped into a dimly lit foyer. The cubicle in which he stood plummeted as numbers glimmered in the air: 100, 200, 300 feet. Bar Far - far from the semi-poisoned shell above. The descending cubicle absorbed sounds: laughter, the clinking of glasses, the rippling of water. The door whooshed open and he walked into an enormous cave. Long black bars stretched on either side. In the middle of this chamber yawned a swimming pool, an underground lagoon. On both ends, the floor sloped to the water's edge, onto a bed of glistening pink sand where the water glowed like zinfandel; and within, four nude women with shaved heads performed what could have been synchronized water ballet. A few older drunken men applauded, tossing coins into the pool, leering as the women raised gleaming vulvas out of the water, swinging their legs wide briefly, before submerging, depth charges of lust. He glanced up and down the upwardly curved, ebony bar, and realized it was shaped like a monumental cock.

Quinton Lent appeared. His skin was the color of garlic but his eyes seemed almost black, as if sapped by this underground world. "Glad you came," he said.

Jonathan said, "Janice Cape must've thought you knew something important."

Quinton grinned stupidly at the police shackle he wore. "She would'a liked me to say that I saw you throw her in the river."

"Who are you exactly?"

"It was my family in who took her in. In Seattle. When she was six."

He imagined that it was Quinton supplied Mitcha with illegal drugs too, like the ones Jonathan once spotted in her refrigerator. Ones they'd used together.

Quinton went on, "My family ain't around no more."

"You want to know who killed her just like I do, right?"

"I got an idea," Quinton Lent said.

"The guy she was involved with, right?"

"I know who she was involved with... You."

"No, no. You don't know me. You told Detective Cape that."

"That is what I told her. That's why we got to talk. I would'a called you but you tapped me first. I lied. Obviously."

Quinton smelled of sweat and urine and the air in this blandly debauched place pressed in. He started to feel ill again. "I…" He steeled himself, hands flat on the bar to stay steady as he waited for a memory, any memory, to flare brightly. But nothing.

Quinton Lent said, "You came up with some, like, bug spray. Big deal."

"It is a big deal when those bugs carried the malaria-Y strain along the Amazon."

"Yep - so there you go. Maybe Mitcha needed someone to talk to but like I told you, we was close in our way."

"That's what you know about me? Just you and a few million other people."

"No, she told me all about you. Professor."

He rubbed his face. "Look, what do you know about what happened to her!"

"Funny thing is, my folks started to like her more than me. I kited away, even before God zero, freak zone material, I admit. When they died, they left everything to our girl. Including their house. I was in no condition, let's surmise. But that's neither here nor there. We fell outta touch for a little bit. But when I found out she was dancin' with the gray angels, I remembered somethin' she said to me. About this particular guy. Which was - she thought he was gonna hurt her."

"Not me."

Was it? Still no memories.

Quinton declared, "In the past, Mitcha was stand-up about money. When I needed it."

"You want money."

121

"I protected you. That cunt was all over me, that cop. You owe me."

"You owe me for wasting my time. Zachariah Willer, he's the one who took off. Why would he do that?"

"Don't even know that name."

"Well, she was seeing him. Shows what you know." Jonathan tapped his fingers on the bar to hide his shaking hand.

"I knew her better than anybody. And I only know you." Quinton Lent's eyelids fluttered. "She told me, she was afraid of the married man."

"She said that? No, you've got it all wrong. It was Willer."

"Go to Tristesse. See what you remember then, fuckwad."

"Tristesse?" He didn't understand this game; couldn't get balanced. "What the hell's that?"

Quinton studied him. "You really don't remember? You don't know?"

"I know… you're full of shit."

"Well, think about how much your home life's worth. Diana's. Henry's. Put a price on it. That's what you'll pay me to keep my mouth shut."

This ragged dialogue had gotten out of hand. He stabbed a finger into Quinton's chest. "Don't ever, ever go near them."

"What're you gonna do, moron? Kill me too?"

He made a fist but forced himself to take a step back - he couldn't risk a violent scene. "I'm surprised they let you in here without hosing you down. Nobody would believe you about anything."

Quinton Lent leaned forward on his elbows, skin pockmarked, breath foul, only the two of them at the bar. "The first time you fucked, you and her, it was in her backyard. You was layin' in the grass. There was an aurora... After she came, she cried."

Jonathan could feel him himself almost physically shrink. "How could you know that?"

"How? Because I was there!"

"What? You were there?"

"She gave me a place to stay, little sis, how nice of her."

There was a room upstairs and someone who listened. Quinton Lent.

He felt defiled, betrayed - ready to lash out but Quinton himself seemed some kind of phantom from the past. "What do you know!"

"You heard what I said. Time's running out. You know where to find me."

"I'm not..." He sought words as his eyes fell and he crimped the end of his bar napkin. He looked up to see that Quinton Lent was gone.

CHAPTER 21

He checked his auto database but there was nothing to indicate "Tristesse" as a programmed destination. He could find no public references to Tristesse at all. Officially, there was no such place.

Meanwhile, the mind-d lay in his pocket of no use now without a charge.

In the Climatology Department at the university, he found a small room off the diorama rotunda. He sat in a padded chair before a raised platform. He asked to speak to Mitcha's thesis advisor.

Dympna Knell, in her sixties, hawk-nosed, in black, appeared. She sat in a gazebo, a stream visible behind her threading into green hills. With its own scenic backdrop, this particular ECO edged left and right as though nudged by uneven winds.

"Hello, Jonathan," the manifestation of Dympna said, looking at him with the same amphibian blankness as his parents. "How's your family?"

"Diana's fine. Henry's fine."

"Your department hasn't been the same since you took your sabbatical. It's in disarray."

"I know." He didn't know anything.

"Since Stillwell retired. I know the Department Chair could be aloof. But he liked you. Now he's Ombudsman."

"Is that right?"

"What can we do for you?" Dympna's ECO asked.

"You were Mitcha Ebrey's advisor -"

"Briefly, last year, yes."

"You knew her well?"

"No. I barely knew her at all. Anyway, you, my friend, look at you. The revolutionary mosquito repellent, swallowed like a fruit drink, balm for the workers in the rainforest."

"I know it's a lot but can you tell me anything about Mitcha's last few months here? Who she hung around with? Where she went?"

"Information has been uploaded to the police."

The personality traits of an ECO still remained a dull mirror of the person. "Have Dympna Knell contact me in person, all right?"

The ECO stated, "If this had been about ten months earlier, you could have talked to Mitcha yourself."

"What do you mean?" Then he realized. "Her own ECO."

"It didn't tell anyone much."

"Has it been permanently deleted yet? Could you..."

The image of Dympna on the gazebo vanished.

He found himself holding his breath. A layer of air fluttered open like tulip petals as if to reveal hidden space behind. Mitcha stood there. It was heart-stopping. She wore a conservative, long, brown suede skirt and high-collared white blouse. The backdrop behind her lay empty - blackness beyond the edge of the universe.

"Hello, Professor."

"You know me," he said, foolishly.

Her ECO would still say nothing but what was departmentally sanctioned. She spoke something so garbled, he couldn't make it out, like rumblings of a flooded gasoline engine. In some other context, it might have seemed comical. He ventured, "Listen, I hope you're happy... Your - your boyfriend Zachariah Willer, he's been bothering you?"

The ECO appeared to be thinking about this, a surge sluggishly rippling the shawl of light. "Oh, Zachariah Willer." The figure threw her head back and laughed. "He's just a boy."

"Yeah, a boy. And - he's no good for you."

"Thank you for your concern."

He pressed his luck. "Isn't he dangerous?"

The ECO didn't respond.

"OK... Quinton Lent, your only living relative, right? What is he doing, Mitcha? He's pressuring you for money?"

"Quinton Lent is one of the unfortunate addicts in our society for whom we must take responsibility. Chemicals will be defeated by chemicals, you and I agree on this. There will be antidotes to all the new addictions, in time."

"You let him into your house, though, didn't you? Maybe he found out things about your private life... What did he find out?"

"What house are you speaking of?"

"The big house where you moved off-campus. Quinton lives with you there sometimes, in a room upstairs."

The ECO didn't react.

"All right, all right... I know you worked with James Martinson. Were you two close?"

The ECO stayed mute, now with a look resembling puzzlement.

126

"Might there have been another person too – say, someone who was Martinson's friend? Someone who wouldn't draw too much attention. Someone who…"

He stopped and listened to deathly silence. His idiosyncratic line of questioning was in vain. Whatever she'd said about Martinson had long since been expunged by some faceless higher-ups to be studied. He broached a new irritating, unanswered question. "If there's someone new in your life, maybe you'd go to Tristesse."

The image appeared to dilute. "I don't know what you mean."

"Well… I don't either," he said, ready to give this up.

Dympna's ECO shimmered to life alongside Mitcha's. "I'm here," she said. Dympna Knell, his old friend - did she want to help him?

"Dympna." Wherever she was physically, she must have been alerted to the conversation. "Who do you think killed her?"

"I can't begin to guess. So horrible. Why are you really here?"

"I don't know, I can't get past it."

"Whatever you say. See Stillwell. Maybe he can help you," she said. "Shouldn't you be taking it easy?"

"Dr. Oskar Rose saved my life and I'm thankful but he can't help me put my life back together… Rose seems to answer to no one."

"Well, there's been a sea change since God-zero. More secrecy. Meantime, you know, many see the medical research community as holding the keys to utopia."

"You have a theory on that?"

"Doctors and scientists like us, you with your super-mosquito repellent, are in the process of eradicating practically all physical diseases or making us immune to them. But policemen have been around for hundreds of years and there's always been and still is crime and terrorism. By changing individual people in their very nature, we can change humankind, goes the thinking."

"Was Martinson working alone?"

"What he cooked up was relatively easy to do, using lab facilities - a powerful synthetic poison. A litre tossed out of a plane disseminated by air currents. A fraction of an inhaled microgram causing death, worse than any botulinum neurotoxin."

"I realize... Well, anyway, I became Dr. Rose's patient in radical organic reconstruction and psychosurgery. Including putting a new coldcell in my head. He said it needs to be there for now but..."

The Dympna ECO began to glow, dawn-gold and dawn-indigo. Surprised, he understood that Dympna herself was conducting a remote scan on his body through the ECO receptors. He lay back, feeling flushed, letting this inspection happen. A minute passed.

Dympna's likeness came back. "Normal functioning, seems. I don't think you should be concerned about anything. What is it you're worried about?"

"Nothing." Everything.

A moment passed. "But something is odd."

He leaned forward. "What?"

"We - for some reason, we can't penetrate the software."

"Meaning, you can't do a functionality scan because you can't get a reading on what the true functions of the coldcell are supposed to be?"

"That's correct."

Dr. Rose's physical, legal and electronic firewalls extended around his entire life and being. "Dympna, what do you think -"

"End of scan... Bye for now." Dympna went off-line. She seemed scared herself.

He didn't know what to do. Mitcha's ECO remained still. "Mitcha? Can you talk to me?" He could have been a dotty widower at a séance.

Mitcha's ECO stood still for a long moment. The program was freezing up or this defunct ECO had nothing else built into it to say, no lingering ability to process. He got up, feeling despair that this was it - that she seemed forever out of reach like his own immediate past.

Mitcha said, "Jonathan, there's something I want to tell you."

My God, he thought - and didn't speak.

"We should meet soon. We need to discuss something. That's all I can say now."

She'd programmed a message before she died. He had no memory of hearing it. But Dympna must have listened to it months ago and was letting him hear it now.

He said, "What date and time is it now, Mitcha?"

"February fourth. 8:41 PM."

The day she was killed.

Mitcha's ECO contracted and vanished.

"Give me other messages, please," he said, maybe to Dympna, maybe to no one.

In a second, a toneless, artificial voice declared, "Final message. Mitcha Ebrey deceased as of February fourth."

Mitcha wanted to contact him the night she was murdered. It seemed the last message she ever sent.

No wonder Cape was coming after him.

CHAPTER 22

Back in the car, he called Stillwell, retired as his Dean, once a chemist for an offshore drilling corporation in the China Sea, who'd been appointed an Ombudsman. In the Canton of Middle New York, the Ombudsman sat as an arbiter of disputes among medical, law enforcement and other local agencies, and a repository of collective information, privy to details that others weren't, ready to share that information with those who could successfully petition for it.

He parked by a dirt path through withered trees, directed here by Stillwell. He trod gummy earth, the woods beyond and the mountains offering a broad-stroked night landscape though it wasn't late. Hidden sensors detected his arrival; Stillwell's home protected its master. When the path opened into a circular clearing, a pod emerged from the dirt, a baby's head from a mossy womb. He stepped in and the pod sank back into the earth. It slid onto a monorail, into a dappled garden in a rainforest. He heard the tranquil drizzle of rain on vegetation on the perimeter, which appeared to stretch for miles lit by a too-white sun, not their own, muted by pastel blue mist.

"Welcome." A stooped, lean old man with wisps of white hair in a vermillion silk robe advanced.

A door opened in a banyan tree, which was a mirage. He followed Stillwell into what became dreary living quarters with old furniture, down a hallway of slate tiles into a too-hot rear room containing two armchairs, a table set with two drinks and surveillance screens of each area of his domain. Stillwell said, "Sit. Raspberry wine?"

"No, thanks."

"What can I do for you, Jonathan?"

"What can you can tell me about the murder investigation of Mitcha Ebrey? It's because of Mitcha's last phone call that Detective Janice Cape assumes I was the last person to see her alive."

"The Canton police have no direct evidence against you."

Jonathan extended his wrist with the police bracelet. "Can you help me with this?"

"No."

"But at least you're telling me that there is no real evidence. Correct? Whatever there might be, it's circumstantial, thin, right? I had no motive, for one thing." He said this though he knew that in the minds of Janice Cape and Quinton Lent he did: he grew jealous of Zachariah Willer, who wanted to reclaim her; or jealous of someone else, someone unknown. "Her boyfriend Willer was a stalker. Plus, she has this odious adopted brother named Quinton Lent. Aren't there any other suspects?"

"Whom would you suggest?"

"Nobody really knows how well she knew James Martinson, how about that?"

"That would be something, to prove a connection at this point."

"I wonder that nothing ever came out about someone who Martinson might've worked with. Someone who had access to lethal materials, who helped him - who also could have known Mitcha.

Someone who might've interceded to keep her quiet. Someone who's still alive."

Stillwell was silent for a moment. "Well... There are always possible loose ends."

"So what do you know about it, sir?"

"You're assuming too much about what I know."

Stillwell gave him a stony stare and went silent. Jonathan said, "Well, - do you know anything about this runt Lent?"

"He's been branded and neutered."

"You indicated he was a suspect too."

"Did he have a reason to kill her?"

"Maybe he did. She put him up at her house. He wants easy cash and he's unhinged. Did she leave anything behind that he would inherit?"

"Less than a quarter acre of land and a hundred year old, rundown suburban ranch house outside Seattle. Nobody's lived in it for years. It belonged to the girl's late adoptive mother. Who was Quinton Lent's biological mother, estranged. It had been left to Ebrey. Do you think that's something to kill for?"

"For him, yes."

"There was no insurance on that. The land is undesirable but he could have laid claim to that house, since she died intestate. If he wanted real estate. So why would he burn down Ebrey's house?"

Stillwell was probably questioning him as much as he was questioning the older man. "I don't know the answer to that, sir."

"Perhaps you can understand frustration of our esteemed Canton police. An impossibly corrupted

133

corpus, degraded DNA. No witnesses. No murder weapon. And this poor unfortunate - almost like a life unlived, so little trace of her left behind."

In his mind, Jonathan couldn't help but see Mitcha's hazel eyes gleaming, looking into his, her smile beckoning as she sat across from him in the college pub. What then seemed a blissful moment - a moment of profound connection between them - now seemed a shadow play.

Stillwell went on, "Her essence was snuffed out with what might even have been some ordinary, un-serrated utility knife."

Jonathan's said more loudly, to keep the doddery Stillwell focused, "Like a knife belonging to one of the Hudson River Hawks. I assume that's obvious too."

"Is it obvious? You might say this is not how a homicide investigation is supposed to go. It's like from another century."

"Well, look, you would have been able to dig up back channel requisitions, like for Kerosote. I assume if you'd been able to determine that I got it, you would've told the cops."

"That's correct, I would have had to. So I don't know... All I can tell you about your lab fire is that an ambulance from the Bluestone Clinic was there in time to save your life. All the debris was disposed of post haste. This has been a common practice since God-zero, when people feared contamination. They still do."

"With all due respect sir, the fire in my lab occurred before God-zero."

Stillwell rubbed his chin. "You make an interesting point. Rose was in a position to make

134

jurisdictional decisions even at that moment in time." He chuckled mirthlessly. "Since God-zero, he has only been able to assume more oversight capacity. He has been encouraged by our leaders. Who, we all know, now serve their automatic twenty-five year terms, with the advent of the New Constitution, since the old one was voided."

"Yes, well, if the explosion wasn't my fault, then no one would know that."

"Are you implying, son, that it was arson?"

"I'm telling you that it can't be ruled out, can it? Maybe it's a long shot but what if Zachariah Willer, Quinton Lent, James Martinson, or even better - some somebody who nobody seems to be looking for! - had tried to kill me too? After murdering Mitcha? Why should that idea be negated? Especially if it turns out that both fires were caused by Kerosote. What you're telling me is that Dr. Rose swept in and there was no investigation into that possibility. And partly, that's why I'm up shit's creek. Sir."

Stillwell took a second then got up and moved to the back wall, which took on a fluorescent glow, his old bones slumping, like having to do this weighed him down. Jonathan focused on a large screen. Stillwell, with his privileged access - one of the reasons he'd come here to begin with - was able to call up the medical file of Dr. Jonathan Kelton. He felt his heart pounding. But this file was sealed, he saw: what the Bluestone Clinic technicians had removed from the wreckage of his lab and then, whatever specific procedures were done to him in the clinic, remained strictly confidential.

Jonathan's file was sub-headed:

135

The Lazarus Experiment.

No other text appeared on the screen, except the number for the file citing the statute under which all this information was protected. "What does that mean, sir?"

"A label for convenience. Self-evident, no?"

"This means that everyone's locked out of the Bluestone Clinic database." It was why Dympna Knell couldn't access information about the coldcell, Jonathan realized. "Even you're locked out."

"Dr. Rose is protecting his multiple pending patents. Something like this has been standard operating procedure when anything experimental is done. It prevents everything from industrial espionage to public outcry."

"But not to this extent."

"Perhaps not. But I'm sure you can appreciate it."

"No, I must say I'm disgusted, sir. Truly disgusted."

Stillwell turned away from him. There was something unusual and Stillwell knew it, Jonathan figured. The code referred to a new technology, that information he could have recited. But normally, medical records would be protected under the rights of the individual, not listed under technology.

On top of everything else, Jonathan, as if to confirm his worst, if wildly inchoate, fears, was not being registered as a person; he was being registered as an invention.

CHAPTER 23

Jonathan pressed on, "Sir, what's Tristesse? I can't find any record of it, or if it's anything at all. Lent mentioned it to me."

"Tristesse... That's not actually what it was called."

"So it is an actual place?"

"It was something else - St. Theresa's. Nicknamed Tristesse for whatever reason. It was a church. An abandoned church."

"A church? Is that all?"

"No. It was turned into a crematorium."

"Crematorium."

"In the town of Gethsemane. In the Sick Zone. To cope with the dead there last year, right after God-zero," Stillwell said.

"I don't know what to make of that. Is there anything else you can tell me?"

"No," Stillwell said. Then, in a second, "We're done now."

He made his way to the door. "Thank you for your time."

He left the old man in this damp, solitary chamber, like a root cellar that hoarded nothing anyone would want, apparently. He trudged back through the dead woods on a path lit with phony, glowing marigold petals.

The building where Claude Jainchill had an office was a dozen stories of mirrored glass. Though he hated doing it, Jonathan checked the distance beforehand to make sure, as he had with each trip, that it was under twenty miles from his home, as he followed up on Wright's instructions to meet with his right-hand man.

Covering his police bracelet with a shirt cuff, he rode a soundless elevator to the top floor, stepping out into a hallway empty but for a dusty fake banana plant. He stepped into a two-room office suite. Jainchill's secretary, a vaguely middle-aged woman with cotton candy pink hair, a tiara-like hairclip and sunken cheeks, was packing things in a purse to go home. She said, "Sit down, all right?" She patted on make-up gazing into a compact mirror, letting out a sigh as a meditation on her looks. The room went uncomfortably silent. Without tables, the one decoration was a bronze statue of Prometheus. The fire-bringer. Some irony there, Jonathan thought. A buzzer sounded on the woman's desk, prompting her to say without looking at him, "Go in now, all right?"

He opened the door to Jainchill's office, a rectangle with gold carpet. There was nothing on the walls. In the light of a long, slender chrome halogen lamp that bisected the room like an awakened snake, he could see that Jainchill, in his sixties, was pale, unshaven and red-eyed, in contrast to his older but robust-looking boss Wright. "Dr. Jonathan Kelton," Jainchill said. He made a weary motion for him to sit in a buttoned-leather chair. "A shame what happened to you."

"I wish I could go back in time to rectify everything," with an unwitting intensity.

"Wouldn't we all."

138

"So you know why I'm here. Mr. Wright wanted me to talk to you. It's imperative I continue working."

"Oh?"

"He believes that... So we can start drawing up a contract to continue to work together."

"Jonathan..." Jainchill clasped his fingers together on his desk edgily, a pile of white worms. "Things are not normal."

"I don't follow."

"My friend, don't be surprised if the company's going under."

"But... how can that be?"

"The patents we've taken to market have not fulfilled expectations."

"But I -"

"You've been out of the loop. Really, you were never in the loop."

"I was a rising star, or so I was told. In our community anyway. Claude, I was."

"How many research scientists are chasing the same dollar? The government can't run itself anymore. Private money isn't available right now, for us."

"The Wright Group funded my home lab."

"And look what happened." Probably, Jonathan's face fell since Jainchill added, "Hey, I'm so sorry, man."

"I want my files back. The back-up file for my inventory."

"I'll see what I can do."

Jonathan stood up. "What do you mean you'll see what you can do?"

"We own your research, that's the deal."

139

"I - I don't believe this is what Mr. Wright wanted."

"Then I'll let him tell you himself."

Wright's ECO appeared in the middle of the barren room. With a coxcomb of white hair and wearing a burgundy vest, the ECO spoke. "Jonathan. We remain deeply sorry about your personal trials. I know you appreciate that we must terminate our agreement, which has lapsed in any case."

"I was hoping for another chance," Jonathan said. So Wright had reneged. "You said –"

The ECO responded with a non-sequitur. "You're in good hands with Dr. Rose, by the way. I know him."

"You know Dr. Rose?" It surprised him that Wright was acquainted with his doctor. But was that of any consequence?

Wright intoned, "All rivers flow to one place. The smart people always knew that. In any event, it's your convalescence that's most important right now. Unhindered by the demands of a new contractual schedule." Wright's ECO smiled vacantly. "Am I right?"

"Sir," Jonathan said, "please transmit all backed up data. Damn it, I need to re-construct what I was working on."

Wright's ECO became the floating image of the company logo, an alembic, an alchemical beaker. It hung in the air as Jainchill said, "I told you, brother, I'll do what I can."

At once, it occurred to him that if he had procured Kerosote - since his formal request had been denied by the college - he would have done it informally at best, illicitly at worst. So he might not have logged in the information with the Wright Group. So he would still not even know from the records of the Wright Group if he'd had it to use.

Jainchill pulled out a small, blue plastic bottle from his desk drawer. It was Eufonia. "Want some? No more worries."

"You too?"

"What?"

"Nothing... No, I don't want any." Jonathan walked to the door. "I'll have to figure out something else then, for work, won't I?"

Behind him, Jainchill grunted. Jonathan opened the door. Jainchill called to him. "Jonathan —"

"Yeah."

"It would've been better if..."

"If what?"

"If... you know, she stayed at the bottom of the river."

He froze at the door for a second but didn't say anything. So he'd become a liability. That was what was new since his meeting with Wright.

Back in the car, Rose appeared on the screen. "What did you think Dr. Stillwell could tell you?"

"I thought he had some powers beyond the police. I thought he could tell me something. So I could help myself."

"You're innocent. Don't you think you are?"

"What do you know about it?"

"I know what Stillwell knows."

"He didn't act like he was on my side."

"Stillwell is not involved in our project. No one else is."

141

"Our project. Me. The Lazarus Experiment."

"You remain the property of the medical system, not the legal system."

"I'm not anyone's property! I know that's what you think, I saw the code. Please tell me more about it."

"He's not on the line," came Diana's voice, with no image on the car screen. "He never was. Honey."

"For Christ's sake." Just when he thought he couldn't feel more demoralized, he found he'd been speaking to some ECO counterpart.

"How'd your tete a tete go?" she asked, sounding as though she was pleasantly drifting within a Eufonia blanket herself.

"I hate to tell you but, uh, the job didn't come through."

"Come see your son. OK? Henry misses you. Just come back. No matter what, this is where you should be, nowhere else."

"That was a blow, Diana. I'm sorry."

"Anyway, for right now we're taken care of by Dr. Rose."

"I don't want to be taken care of by Dr. Rose. Look, I'll be right there."

On his block, the thought came to him that he didn't have any memory of his own neighbors either. But maybe he never knew them - one house a mustard-yellow series of turrets with a rococo iron gate, the next a two-story, irregular trapezoid the color of vermouth, on Sahara-like, fluid plastic dunes like a big sandbox, these blighted fortresses.

He saw that an ambulance had parked in front of his own necrotic lawn. It sat red and white in a warhead shape, with its jelly-like energy field overhanging and looking predatory - ready to haul him away, forcibly if necessary. So this was Rose's new tactic and the basis of his warning just now.

A motorcycle with a protective screen, like an upside down canoe, shot down the street. Jonathan parked a couple of houses away from his own to observe a small, hunched man clambering off to ring his doorbell. It was Quinton Lent. With wraparound sunglasses and hands in pockets of a windbreaker, Quinton maneuvered to the casement window of Jonathan's house and sneaked a look inside. A guy rushed out of the ambulance to stop him. Quinton's jaw dropped at the window. The paramedic, a hulking figure in a white, full-body suit with facemask, looking like some rampaging beekeeper, grabbed him, injecting him with something resembling a knitting needle. Quinton stumbled away, drooling, and staggered towards his motorcycle - whipping out a piece of paper. He looked at Jonathan - Quinton saw him. He was sending him a note. The motorcycle roared away, carrying its almost incapacitated rider as he let the paper drop from his fingers, gliding into a gutter three houses away. The paramedic watched it. Jonathan snatched up the paper from the street before the other man could. Affixed to this scrap was an aspirin-sized button.

He tapped it and Quinton's recorded voice spoke: "Who you are will infect you."

Jonathan shouted, "What is this, this is bullshit! Prove to me you know something. What about Tristesse?"

No answer came.

He asked the paramedic what the intruder said to him and the man replied nothing. He informed Jonathan he was armed with a stun gun and assigned by Rose to prevent anyone from loitering or interfering in any way.

He burst into his house and found Diana and Henry sitting in the living room. She glared at him. He said, "Some guy was spying, didn't you see that? He came up to the window."

Diana stood up and looked outside. "Jonathan, what happened?"

"We don't let strangers in the house," Henry said.

Jonathan hid Quinton Lent's note in his hand, as Henry watched him, pursing his lips. "You're right, Henry." Diana was giving Jonathan a stern look. He tried to change his own mindset on the spot, as he caught his breath. "I missed you guys. Henry... Can I talk to you for a little while?"

Henry nodded eagerly. He ushered the boy outside. They sat at the patio table under a hemisphere of tinted glass.

"A man tried to get into our house?" Henry asked.

"No, it was nothing. No one could get in anyway. This house is very safe."

Henry looked wistful to him, and oddly, more like a diminutive man as he sat, leaning forward thoughtfully, face crinkled as if with weariness. "Which house do you like better, Daddy, this one or our other one?"

He could see that other house in his mind - a cottage on a flat, exposed tract on Long Island. Small, crustacean-like ships of the Unity Party

144

militia had patrolled the waters, docking nearby in ports where rotted fishing boats had been left to be consumed by the sea, even in those days before God-zero, fraying on vulnerable environmental fringes. He saw crushed clamshells on the shore, brownish, bubbly sea foam slapping over itself to slither in and pool at his bare feet. He suddenly missed that house - missed that time, again. "I like both houses."

"The other house had a swing set," Henry said.

He saw a glaze in Henry's eyes that matched Diana's, he thought, from the Eufonia. "Well, I'll build a swing set right here."

"Remember how you used to push me, Dad?"

"Sure."

"We went higher and higher..." Henry made a gesture, with rising hands. "But then, that one time, I fell off, I couldn't stop, I couldn't hold onto anything... I flew off."

"But you were OK, right?" A truncated memory of that came back as well. He gave Henry a hug. "You were OK."

"I fell on my arm. I hurt it. I couldn't feel it for a long time."

"That wasn't fun."

He wanted to ask Henry about things he liked now, his favorite subjects, but to act like he didn't know would only further alienate or confuse the boy. "Hey, I'd love to throw a baseball around tomorrow, what about you?"

"Yeah... Can you help me with trigonometry later?"

"Sure I can."

"Love you, Dad."

145

"I love you too."

"I'm gonna go inside now, OK?"

"OK." Jonathan turned around to see Diana staring at them from the kitchen window. For some reason, she looked frightened.

Jonathan didn't find her inside, though, as Henry went to his room.

Who you are will infect you, Quinton had said. What did he really know, anything? Wasn't this a juvenile taunt and a bluff?

With so much still dismally blank in his own mind, feeling raw and depleted, in the living room, he slipped a disk into the projector from January last year, the month before his fire. He wondered if there was some way the double life he'd led with Mitcha had bled through - how he'd acted, if he'd mentioned where he went in his free time, anything he said to his wife and son - even how he looked. Were there drug effects, some types of small scars even?

In one of the last recordings of himself before the fire, he viewed himself standing in his garage, lugging a bottle like a big water jug, jumping with mosquitoes, for testing. But he dropped it clumsily and the bottle lost its seal, so the bugs flew out. They looked to be bouncing themselves off the wall and, in some synchronous dance, Diana spun with the bugs as they swirled around her. He turned the overhead air conditioning unit to high so the mosquitoes got sucked in and spit out in small wafers that fluttered to the floor like black rain.

No archives remained of the interior of his lab, he'd already concluded, which would have been helpful, to see if he stored small amounts of Kerosote.

He found a disk dated from only two days before the explosion in his lab. Other images appeared in front of him. A family vacation. In this movie, it appeared that he and at other times Diana had flicked on some tiny floating camera. It wound up forming a haphazard chronology, neither of them having paid much attention to the filming.

Three days before the fire, he and Henry loaded up the six-seater with a tent and supplies. To ensure everyone would be comfortable, he passed around a bottle of his new mosquito repellent. Mosquitoes had been found festering in some of the low-lying swamps, Jonathan said on camera, as if making an official announcement.

The man in the movie acted scattered and aloof. That Jonathan spooned his formula into six-year-old Henry's mouth, who puckered and the liquid dribbled down his chin. Diana, for her part, swilled it right from the bottle. Neither his wife nor son had ever taken it before.

Then they were off.

The camera shut for a brief interlude then flickered back to life in the car, which sped down the Thruway, the vehicle trailing someone's single scarlet taillight, looking like it raced a drop of blood down a bottomless well. Their car veered off the highway - probably no one even remembered the camera was on, it - past a thicket, onto a dirt path that once lay paved but was allowed to sink into loam. It bumped forward and they passed a sign: Gethsemane. This was the town Stillwell had referred to.

In the movie, someone's hand waved in front of the camera and turned it off. But a night bird squawked and seemingly set off the camera again at an odd angle off the ground. The sound of crickets erupted from out of the dead shapes of the mountains. In a grove of blue spruce, tremulous in a night breeze, Jonathan had cooked a steak in a hibachi and they sat watching the fat drip from the griddle, spattering and quickening the flames.

From his armchair, now, he could hear the slurp of lake water against cracked logs wedged on the shore.

Camera dark.

He waited. Nothing more. He shut off the movie.

They must have returned home the following day, about two days before the fire in his lab.

No records existed from after this day. And this footage didn't tell him anything definite; records tantalizingly elusive as his own blown-out memory. If Tristesse did hold secrets of its own, they had to be buried in those woods.

CHAPTER 24

In the bathroom, he splashed his tired eyes with water. The implants were too perfect to become bloodshot but they still ached in their sockets. His neck got pinched and he tried to squelch the pain with his hand. Diana stood behind him withdrawing a syringe. "What the -?"

"We missed a shot."

"Why do you have to do that?"

"I told you, doctor's orders." She wagged a finger in the air, in an uncharacteristically theatrical gesture. "You want your intestines to start oozing out?" Her curls still held a stylish shape and subtle blue-black eye shadow gave her eyes a sensual, more elongated look - she'd been spending time all along making herself up, he thought. But her perceptions seemed fractured.

He became momentarily light-headed and dazed from the drug. He dropped onto the couch. "Don't do it again without alerting me."

"Sorry. What do you want for dinner?"

"Anything you make is fine."

"We have chicken."

It was what they'd had the past two nights. "Fine."

"What was so important that you had to go running around in the middle of the night?"

"Dr. Rose hasn't been able to help me with the memory loss, I thought you realized that."

"All Dr. Rose has done is help you."

"To help me, Dr. Rose has someone guarding our house. What about that?"

"That's your own fault."

On the couch, his body sagged. "Look, you realize what it means that I'm under house arrest. Diana. I have to be able to counter what somebody like this idiot Quinton Lent, this guy that came to the house, might be saying about me. I have to - you know, try to stay one step ahead somehow. If I even can."

She hovered above him. "Dr. Rose is still keeping the cops away. That god-awful woman."

"But how long can he do that?... Wait, maybe you think I'm guilty of something too. If there's anything you want to tell me..."

"What?"

"I don't know... I mean, I'm sorry if I ever hurt you in some way -"

"What do you mean by that?"

"Physically?"

"No."

"Henry either?"

"No."

He felt reassured. "Look, you really don't know if I was home the whole night on February fourth of last year, or the morning of the fifth? You said I was always working and you never saw me. But were we with each other during that time - don't you know that?"

"I'll say whatever I need to say, if I have to, that's not an issue either."

"No. I'm asking you for the truth."

He waited with anxiety for her to tell him. Her gaze wavered. "The truth?" she said. "The truth is that I don't remember."

He let out a slow breath.

"You had your lab and I was just beginning my project," she went on. "Sometimes we wound up in bed at the same time, sometimes we didn't. You fell asleep downstairs. If you went out, I wouldn't even know. If you came back, I probably wouldn't hear you... Those days just - they seem a blur now."

"Sounds bad."

"Not bad. It just was."

"But... You don't recall seeing anything out of the ordinary?"

"Like what? You standing there, holding a bloody knife?"

"Jesus Christ, Diana, come on, you know what I'm saying, anything... About how I – I might've looked, what I was doing...."

"I don't recall seeing anything odd."

"OK."

"Don't you understand?" she said, "That's why I believe you had nothing to do with this business."

In unfamiliar places inside him, knots unclenched. "OK. That is something... Thanks."

"Jon... What we had in the beginning - we have it back now."

She stretched out her hand and he held it. "Yes... Being together with you and Henry, that's all that matters now."

He looked into her eyes, which got suddenly teary. Then she smiled and walked into the kitchen.

"But neither one of us knows what I was really doing," he muttered, to himself. Mitcha had called

151

him right before she was killed. Wouldn't he have had some involvement in, or at least some knowledge about, the events of February 4th and 5th?

Before he got blown up - and should've died too.

Except for the Lazarus Experiment that saved him. That remade him.

He found it hard to face Diana again, since he was neither lying nor being truthful, just talking. He lumbered upstairs. In the bedroom, he grabbed for the mind-d in the drawer.

"Hi, Daddy."

He spun around as Henry strolled blithely into the bedroom. "Hi."

Henry sat on the bed and nuzzled him. The boy picked up the mind-d. "What's this?"

He lifted it out of Henry's fingers and slipped it back into his pocket. "This?"

"Somethin' to help you?"

Henry rested his head on his knee. "Yeah. Somethin' to help me."

"Sorry I talked about my hurt arm before."

"You can say anything you want to me. Any time."

"Sometimes I can't control what I say."

"What? Henry?" He cupped the boy's chin and looked into his crystalline blue eyes. "I like everything you say. Maybe you can even sometimes help me remember things I forget. Don't ever be afraid to talk to me."

Henry burrowed his head into a pillow. Reassuring his son in such an empty way only made him feel more miserable.

He would have to get the mind-d to work again to give those words weight.

In minutes, he left Henry sleeping in the bed. He found Rose waiting for him at the bottom of the stairs. Out the living room window, he saw the sky turning red, a pyroclastic cloud of crimson swirling out of the volcano mouth of the setting sun. It was the winter sky bleeding through Rose's face that told him that the doctor was not really there, even as the doctor's voice said, "It's taken a turn for the worse outside."

"Thanks for the weather report. I know I can't get away from you, you don't have to keep proving it to me. I'm not doing anything I don't think I can handle."

"You don't know what you can handle."

"What is it you want me to do, doctor?"

"I want you to sit still."

"There is no healing unless I feel I'm helping to heal myself. Can you understand that? Please?"

"I can make you sit still."

"I won't let you. Not you or your guard." He said this knowing that he wouldn't be able to prevent it.

This version of Dr. Rose didn't go away. But he sidestepped the hovering Rose figure, while pellets of ice burst against the living room window like buckshot. He hurried to the garage, the mind-d in his pocket, to venture into the unknown.

CHAPTER 25

He accessed the database of the cramped white six-seater, retrieving information about the camping trip to the Adirondacks that had carried them in this car through the Sick Zone and past the town of Gethsemane, as he'd just glimpsed in the home movies.

In his Ford, next to that car, he could tap into the backup voltage pan. That was where he could find a new source of energy for the mind-d. He unscrewed a circuit tray from under the dashboard.

He drove out, emerging from the garage as this new storm hammered the earth. He checked the mirror to see if the ambulance carrying Rose's lone guard followed him. Naturally, it did. But it didn't race after him. Hail ricocheted through glassy fog but his car didn't waver. He traveled the route he once did with his family.

In twenty minutes or so, his vehicle decelerated. It came to rest on a mound of frozen mud. The car couldn't advance by itself - there were no disks in this road to guide it. He sat in the front seat amidst a contained mess of tools and circuits. He plugged the mind-d into the small, detached voltage pan. He watched the nodule spark to life, glowing like a match. He hesitated then tucked it behind his ear, clasping it to his hair so it hugged his skin hotly like before. Then he drove manually down this creek of ice, passing a bent sign with washed-out print barely visible: Gethsemane.

A tall, metal fence blocked his entrance - a manmade wall sealing off the skeletal forest.

Tristesse sat somewhere within.

One gate stood open, fresh tire tracks visible. It looked like someone else had been here too. He proceeded through the gate into a copse webbed with fog, amidst the hail.

The newly charged mind-d still didn't kick in.

Earlier, he'd come upon a flare gun he kept in the glove compartment, which would be good in case he got stranded. But here he was in the middle of an ice storm, willing to risk getting lost in the woods, playing with random energy. Did he know what he was doing? Wasn't it just blind desperation? But for what?

To know himself.

To save them all.

The broken road gave out. He continued over rocky stubble, which suddenly opened, surprisingly, into what looked like a tarmac. The banging hail softened on his car roof, becoming more like a febrile autumn rain. Heat was being generated here, melting the hail in mid-air. He found that he sat under a jellyfish bubble; a sterile energy field like that which enclosed the ambulance that was on his trail.

The mind-d tickled him at first, then this became an animal bite - and finally, as before, like a steady nipping of flame on the skin. He wanted to rip it off but didn't, instead gripping the steering wheel, sweat trickling between his shoulder blades.

What was here to remember!

Headlights switched on far off and he saw a white van on the edge of the tarmac. The van moved toward him. There was writing on the side, blue letters in bold script. Bluestone Clinic.

Had the doctor just alerted other clinic people? No, trucks were here already, he saw, a battery of them. So the Sick Zone, with it Tristesse, had been taken over by the Bluestone Clinic. By Dr. Rose. What did that mean?

His skull felt squeezed and his car vibrated like a bell...

He opens his eyes to what appears to be a bloated red moon but seen through a prism. He's looking through cracked stained glass, high above him, both of them lying on some cold, hard pallet. Mitcha's usual purple lipstick has turned brown and cracked at the corners of her mouth.

He hears some kind of pounding far off, measured yowls of pain.

In the damp air, she pulls off her panties in a single movement with her thumb. A tiny device appears in her hand, the one that looks like a taser. She sticks him with it, inducing a shock - the effect is like strafing his ganglia, bright fires erupting in his head. Naked, he pushes himself into her. Her legs slap around him, growing tighter as she arches up. He releases in a dizzying rush, magenta spots behind his eyes like a brilliant storm of flower petals.

A thimble-like attachment on her forefinger screws into the soft of his back, releasing something coldly thrilling into his veins, an orgasmic afterburn. He watches his own blood wend its way down her legs - the two of them as if breaking together, like figures melting in a kiln.

Wails come from above. People are watching him and Mitcha from a choir loft. Some onlookers wear colored scarves to cover their faces, some leather masks, looking like the condemned.

Someone throws something at them - cool, little stones or marbles - taking tiny bites out of his back as he lies on top of her, conjoined, what seems to him in this second one single, glorious wound -

His eyes shot open.

Tristesse.

That was what it was like. This place now moldering in the foul darkness of a devastated town. It was some arena for rites of flagellation, masochism, sadism...

Now, he was looking at the inside of his own garage. Out of breath, he lay back in the driver's seat of his Ford. The interior sat warm, intact as though he'd never disassembled it - as though he'd imagined the whole foray. He checked his watch - 7: 42 PM - about an hour after he went out. Dr. Rose's faceless workers must have helped his car return him here.

He looked to his right to see the apparition of Dr. Rose in the passenger seat, like his ECO just wriggled back through a portal in the automobile. Jonathan said, "So part of the Sick Zone, where Tristesse was, has been closed off by the Bluestone Clinic. Why?"

"For soil and water samples. It was dangerous because of God-zero. People who passed through were becoming symptomatic. It was a safety matter."

Dr. Rose had allowed him to see it - he'd let this happen. "Is that really all there is to it?"

"Yes."

"I don't believe you."

"You're looking at the wrong things."

"What do you mean? You lied to me about Tristesse, you told me you didn't know anything about it."

"No, I didn't. I said I know what Stillwell knows. The church is still there. But only its structure."

"It was used as a crematorium?"

"It had been used as that temporarily, out of necessity, right after God-zero. There was a good deal of panic at that time. Some ignorance. About whether infected bodies could be transported out of the Sick Zone, for fear of contamination, or whether they even could be buried in the soil."

"But before that, people went there, whether you or Stillwell know it or not -"

"Whatever people did, it has nothing to do with what's going on there now."

He thought that he and Mitcha had acted out something violent and quasi-ritualistic at Tristesse. When it ceased being an active church as St. Theresa's, it had become an outlandish, maybe secret sex club. So that was what she'd wanted. God help him, he'd begun to want it too, there seemed no doubt about it, now. The drugs were there to make it feel good.

Yet these activities didn't necessarily have a hand in her death.

Did they?

He said, "I went there. To Tristesse, before God-zero."

"How can you be sure what the mind-d is sending you is even real, Jonathan?"

"How?... It is."

This ECO went away.

He pushed open the car door and near-staggered into the house. Diana stood in the living room. He tried to stand upright in front of her but he weaved, with self-hatred overwhelming him. He made it easy for her to inject him again, just let her do it. "I wish..." he said.

She looked confused herself, though calm.

He gave her what he thought was an impish grin but maybe he just looked insane. "I wish... things had been different."

"Jon, all I know is that you were crazy enough to go out again and Dr. Rose got you back here."

"Did he tell you where I went?"

"He knows you're trying to jar your memory."

"You do see why I have to, don't you?"

"Jon... Even if - even if something happened - if something did happen between you and this girl... We can't let it affect us now! For Henry's sake at least... No matter what, you aren't that person anymore."

"Diana, my God..." Was she giving up on ever trusting him fully? Had that already happened? Was it better if he never remembered!

He fell against the banister. Diana lugged him up the stairs.

Ice had taken over outside, he saw.

Some ferocious animal smell hoisted him awake, a violent stink. He made his way to the next room, Henry's, stopping to catch his breath. Rain hit the window and vaporized teeth of ice. The

159

hallway felt uneven, his body listing like a ship in the storm. He saw a bloody handprint stamped on the door. A vinegary trail led across the parquet floor to the bed. A mound lay under a red tangle of sheets, with vapors of faeces and blood.

He thought it looked like... no! Henry had been hacked to death.

CHAPTER 26

His son lay mutilated, upside down in a foul backwash, hand touching the floor in a fist as if poised to strike an intruder.

Jonathan stumbled to the stairs, limbs shaking. "Help!"

Diana appeared at the top of the stairs, clutching a tumbler of whisky. She didn't seem to know what happened. How was that possible! "Diana…" He tried to put one foot in front of the other but pitched forward and took a helpless tumble. At the bottom of the steps, Diana bent over him.

His awareness flickered out.

He awoke to her banging on the dresser with the handle of a hairbrush. When she stepped away, he saw his mind-d cracked into pieces. She jerked his wrists as he tried to swim free in the bed but foundered. She tied his hands and feet with leather cords. Then she exited the bedroom.

"Help him!" Through the diamond-shaped window, he viewed the retreating storm. "Diana!"

Silence answered him. He wept, trapped in the bed.

It wasn't Diana but Dr. Rose who appeared at the door. "Henry -" was all Jonathan could get out.

Rose gave him an injection of some kind and his shaking ceased. The doctor undid the leather cords. Jonathan climbed out of bed and ran into Henry's room. His son's bed sat empty and neatly made. No blood. "Where is he!"

161

"Henry's fine," Rose said. "He's at the oculum now. Baseball practice."

"What! Is he all right!"

"He is."

"Baseball…" It was where Henry said he'd be, earlier. Had he just imagined it? How - ?

Rose, eyes looking overtired and bloodshot, put an arm, thick and lumpy as a rump roast, around his shoulder, the doctor's breath hot. This was Rose himself, not some ECO. "Your son's perfectly all right."

He waved his hand to indicate the room. "But - blood all over the goddamn place…"

"Jonathan, what you saw wasn't there."

"But… I want to see Henry!"

"Diana's gone to get him," the doctor said softly.

"It was so real! I felt his blood, smelled it - right here."

He took a long breath, Rose's tranquilizer bathing his half-unreal flesh. He glanced out the bedroom window. Janice Cape's car was parked right outside. It sat in an odd face-off, as if in some animal wordlessness, with Rose's vehicle not twenty feet away across the street. The front door opened and Diana walked in, Henry behind her, wearing soiled gym clothes and a baseball glove. Jonathan hurried down the steps, letting out a weird laugh. He grabbed his son as warm relief surged through him, like his sundered being flowed back together.

"Hi, Dad." Henry wrapped his mitt hand around his father, returning his embrace clumsily.

162

"I love you, Henry" Jonathan said to his son, again.

"I believe you, Dad."

He kissed Henry on top of the head and held his lips to his son's sweaty hair for a long time.

Later, while Henry was washing up in the bathroom, Jonathan asked Diana, "What's wrong with me?"

"I don't know."

"You smashed my mind-d."

"You were killing yourself with it." Her fingers darted in different directions for a second. "You fell down the stairs."

"So after you destroy some technology of immeasurable value, you tie me to the bed like in some nineteenth century asylum. That's what you do."

Rose interceded. "She did what I told her to do. I thought that thing was inconsequential at first. It was crucial for you to feel you had freedom. But I gave you too much. I waited too long, it was a mistake."

"But I - I was remembering." He almost blurted out that half-formed, execrable memory of Tristesse but stopped himself.

"What you just experienced was a nightmare that could've killed you," Rose said. "Your brain is rebelling, can't you see that?"

"No - what if - maybe this nightmare was telling me something."

"What in God's name do you think it was telling you?" Diana's voice cracked. She stood there still wet from the rain, stringy hair clinging to ice-sheen cheeks.

163

She and Rose watched him as he settled into a chair. In spite of himself, he longed for the blanketing balm of sleep. He closed his eyes, drifting within himself, liquid within liquid. "I..." He could barely complete a thought. "Doctor, what are you doing to me?"

"This is nothing I've done," Rose said somberly.

"You - you think this just happened... because of the mind-d."

Rose tapped his fingers anxiously. "Obviously, dream-renderings aren't literal. They're distorted manifestations of our fears. Dramatizations, if you will."

"But someone's dead for real, cut up, in a way like I just saw. Mitcha Ebrey."

"Your pre-existing psycho-chemistry pushed you into this tactile experience. Interesting. The coldcell might have contributed to that. Call it 'hard dreaming.' All right. But your obnoxious little mind-d started working disjointly with the coldcell. I never thought it could happen but it wound up causing some kind of mental convulsion, finally."

But if it was just a nightmare "externalized," couldn't it still have been sending a message to him, in some kind of dream-language?

"Look... maybe - maybe everybody's at risk now," he said. He couldn't help but think, as he said to Stillwell, that someone could have tried to kill both him and Mitcha separately; somebody else who'd obtained Kerosote. Maybe someone was trying to kill them all. Wasn't that possible? Then, was what he just experienced not just a dream howling in the light of day but, yes, maybe something more like a premonition? That was what was brought on by the mind-d. "Listen…"

Rose interrupted him. "I own a villa on Lake George. It's peaceful and protected."

"You don't," he uttered, "understand…" He was eager to try to force some substance onto what did seem like shattering, momentary lunacy. But his mind was turning into a river to nowhere. "Yeah, good deal, right, Diana and Henry, you know, need a break."

"No one else will know where they are," the doctor said. "I can make sure of that. Otherwise, this grotesque detective will continue to interfere in your lives. For the moment, she can prevent you from traveling there because of house arrest."

"Hah, you think you can do everything… but you couldn't - why didn't you help me with remembering? Can you… can you… do it?" He started giggling.

"You'll be reunited with your wife and son soon," Rose said, his voice unbending iron.

Jonathan caught sight of Henry whisking by, hustling up the stairs to his bedroom, seemingly oblivious. Jonathan was gladdened by that, the boy seemed unsuspecting about what happened to him.

The guard entered from outside wearing his white full-body gear. He and the doctor each grabbed one of Jonathan's arms, for some reason. He felt the fly bite of another injection and nose-dived into sleep. Sad, dead weight in their arms.

CHAPTER 27

Under the crisp, white sheets of his own bed, he felt misshapen and swollen-headed. Diana came into his line of sight and smiled. Henry appeared beside her. "Hi, Daddy," Henry said. "You OK?"

"Yes... I am."

"Kiss Daddy good-bye," she said to Henry.

Henry leaned over and his wet lips touched Jonathan's cheek. He smiled at his son. "Bye, Daddy."

"Bye for now. See you soon."

"Bye for now," Henry repeated.

"We'll just be gone a few days," she said, though he realized she couldn't know for sure, none of them could.

He shut his eyes groggily, as he heard them shuffle out. Would they miss him? Did Diana resent him now? The burden of him. Why Rose had to take them away. What a shame that there would have to be more separation. What a goddamn shame... Because of him - because of things he caused.

These thoughts became diffuse like silt.

When he opened his eyes, the room was empty and dark. He made his way to the rosewood dresser. He yanked open drawer after drawer to see what was there. Diana had packed most of her clothes. So Rose planned a long absence for her and Henry, after all. But maybe that was for the best. Diana would not be harassed and Henry would not have to wake up each morning to the sight of a cop car parked outside.

He spread the drapes on the bedroom window, propping himself against the window frame. There they were. Janice Cape's police vehicle and Dr. Rose's medical transport still parked in front of his house, waiting for him for different reasons, on opposite sides of the street. He saw this round-the-clock police surveillance as unnecessary but probably a tactic to unnerve him – a blatant show of force perhaps designed to push him into a confession.

He went downstairs to the rec room where Diana had spent so many hours - this windowless, sterile-looking space with a bare wood floor, where she built her model of a medieval convent and church. He couldn't escape seeing a connection to Tristesse though none existed. It didn't take long before he got her project to reconstruct itself. It bounced from floor to ceiling, within a cocoon-like and enveloping, specially-treated, invisible scrim. A fabric of light pleated within and then away from him in great swaths, billowing out and looking to stiffen, to stretch for a hundred feet or more in a room only 20'X12'. This never quite looked real, however all-encompassing. Still, he heard chanting far off in Latin, female voices pianissimo in an interior trapped in degrees of twilight. Diana had done a workmanlike job. She was more technically sophisticated than he'd given her credit for.

He thought again that he should have included her in discussions of his own work. How much that would have helped him in his predicament now.

167

He advanced up the central aisle of her Gothic cathedral, which swooped upwards in a vaulted ceiling. It looked higher than it ever could have been in reality, soaring and becoming tissue-y around the edges, sticks of light unable to quite support the girth of this illusion. He stood still, air tight in his lungs. He wondered if this could jog his memory further about Tristesse, without the mind-d.

Nothing came up,. He shut the model down. He felt winded though he'd done so little. Something caught his attention out the bedroom window - a stucco A-frame right across from his, where a round window shone rose-pink, electronically tinted, like a diseased eye peering at him. An eye into places inside him that he couldn't reach himself, he thought absurdly. Someone had been watching him through that window from across the street then activated the blinds.

Someone who might have witnessed other comings and goings, like on the fateful day of his lab explosion.

The street outside lay empty but for Rose's and Cape's vehicles. He confirmed the A-frame as the only one with an unobstructed view of his whole house, including the outer perimeter of his backyard where the oblong metal box of his lab had once stretched. Across the street, he trod a concrete walkway that lay fissured, as if each home sat behind its own little fault line, in its own zone of upheaval. He tried to fight off his jittery fatigue, dragging him into anxiety and inadequacy. But despite his mushroom pallor and thinness, in a crew-neck, burgundy wool sweater and jeans, he thought he looked OK, normal. He knocked. A wrinkled Amazon of a woman almost seven feet tall, amber hair in a bun, peeped out.

"I'm Dr. Jonathan Kelton. I live across the street." She grimaced but surprisingly, let him right in. "Thanks. I was hoping I could speak to you."

"I know who you are. You came out of the fire."

"Yes."

Inside a pristine room with white wall-to-wall carpeting and a glass table, she gestured for him to sit on a plum-colored couch with fringed pillows. Some moody orchestral piece played. She silenced the strings with a voice command.

"Do you live here alone?"

She looked poised to run away from him if she had to. "Since my Richard died."

He noticed the left wall glimmering faintly - a phantom presence. She would no doubt talk to her late husband about this later. It appeared their world was increasingly peopled by the half-dead, the half-sane. He gave a nod to the wall before the illumination faded out. What form did Richard take, he couldn't help but wonder? He knew some people chose a hovering light to give the sense of the essence of spirit. "I forgot your name, I'm sorry."

"My name is Adele Arancia. Why did you come here?"

"Obviously, you can see my house from here, you have a clear view - I'm wondering if you've ever seen anything suspicious."

"Suspicious? Like what?"

"I don't know, like a stranger to the neighborhood, somebody you never saw before. Somebody doing something out of the ordinary."

She seemed to be running the question through her head. "I…"

"Anything at all?" he pressed.

"I don't spy on people."

"No, of course not." His sense of purpose deflated. If Mrs. Arancia hadn't even glimpsed Quinton Lent in his blatant intrusiveness recently then what might she ever have seen? "But it looked like you were about to say something."

In a second, she said, "I'm here alone with Richard."

"I… don't know what you mean by that."

"Nobody to protect me."

"You're scared of something?"

"I'm not a snoop, Dr. Kelton. People think I'm watching them because I'm very tall."

"No, nobody would think that. Anybody can see you're a - a good person."

"Yes. I am a FACT."

In a droll coincidence, he happened to have glimpsed that on a bumper sticker on a car: Found Again Christian Traditionalist. "I appreciate that you are."

"Not a theory. A FACT."

"Which means you're a good citizen too. You would always be helpful if you could. The police are right outside. You would be protected. From anyone. For any reason."

"Like they protected that girl?"

"Mrs. Arancia… what are you afraid of?"

He grabbed her. "What is it you have to say?"

170

She recoiled. "Music!" she yelled. Dark rumblings swelled again. She walked out of the room.

He dreaded stepping back outside, to a vacant house, into his own void. He spoke louder over the music, "Mrs. Arancia, I think you wanted to tell me something. Please!"

The lights dimmed around him until he sat on the plum-colored couch in near-darkness, waiting for her to respond. Whatever she wanted to say earlier, now she wanted him to leave.

Nobody was telling him anything. Janice Cape, wide-brimmed, brown hat pulled low, again stood waiting for him at the end of the dirt-encrusted, buckled walkway. The beekeeper-looking figure emerged from Dr. Rose's vehicle in yet another odd standoff, positioning himself in the road yards away from him and Janice Cape like in an Old West showdown. In this instance, it seemed Cape who might protect him from Rose. "Learned anything new?" he asked her.

"What'd you learn from your neighbor?"

He bluffed. "You know. You talked to her too."

He watched over Cape's shoulder as Rose's guard observed them silently and stepped forward. Jonathan coughed. "Listen, I don't like this air. If you want to talk privately, let's do it."

"Hop in, Cape said.

He did. As soon as the door to the police car closed, he regretted it.

171

CHAPTER 28

Cape said, "I want to talk to your wife."

"Diana and our son have gone on vacation."

"I thought it might be something phony like that." Cape, haggard, her round belly spilling over her belt, massaged her temples. She sat in the back seat face to face with him as the car pulled out on its own. The settling evening burst with lemon-colored sparks, minimal sky traffic, Canton patrols, lending backlight to puffballs of fog. He could see up close that Cape's overly malleable fingers weren't completely natural and for the first time, he noticed a ridge of flesh perforating her wrist. She saw him looking. "Just thought it was candy in a kid's hand. Didn't know it was a bomb. Some punk out to get a cop."

"Oh. Too bad... Listen, Diana and Henry have been through so much already -"

"I'm sure they're OK. What is it about Eufonia?"

So Cape had discovered that Diana was taking it and probably Henry too; their private lives had been breached by the police.

"I don't know, I never tried it."

"You know, with all this sitting and watching, I never actually saw your son at all. What's his name again?"

"His name is Henry."

"I like that name, by the way. Like one of my favorite writers. Henry David Thoreau. Ever hear of him?"

172

"As a matter of fact, that's why we named him, Diana and me. Henry David, that's his name." He tried to force a smile and it didn't work. "I minored in American literature. But you knew that, didn't you?"

"No one at his school has seen your son either, by the way."

"What do you mean?"

"Henry David's a mystery kid. Been attending special private classes, arranged by the Bluestone Clinic. 'Cause of post-traumatic disorder after the fire at your house, blah blah blah. That's what I was told. And we know that nobody gets to see what goes on at the Bluestone Clinic."

He squirmed in the car seat. He knew Cape noticed it. Diana should have told him this. Or maybe he just should have assumed Henry would be under special care. That made sense - he'd observed that Henry didn't seem to be properly socialized, Eufonia or not. He said, "Good. For the best."

They drove in silence. Before long, Cape led him into an elevator, fake teakwood polished to a mirror shine, which opened on to the third floor at the center of a hub. A series of narrow corridors branched out from this circular vestibule. This police station had an air of bygone elegance, with its pointed, egg yolk-yellow ceilings with Art Deco scalloping, paint cracking now, and molding that consisted of thin tubes of sky-blue light, once in style. It was built at a time when full-scale modernization of the police force was a great public works project, he reflected as the two of them advanced - when the first standardized system of

173

identification through gene-complete DNA fingerprinting for each member of the population was instituted. Everyone's DNA was on file. It was assumed no homicides would go unsolved or unpunished nor would the wrong man ever be accused; no longer would bodies go unclaimed or missing children be untraceable. So much for that.

He saw in one hallway that a skinny kid with a shaved head lay naked, writhing. He bore a tattoo on his forehead like Quinton Lent. Two male, black cops in open collar, white dress shirts watched him, chuckling. It did seem unfortunately comical until he saw that half of the man's face had been cut away, hanging blubbery and blood-soaked.

"Comin' down," Cape remarked. "Smashed a mirror, sliced off pieces of his face with the broken glass - started feeding the strips of skin to his pit bull. The supercrank grains, they stay dormant, explode when you least expect it. Voila."

She nudged him into an office. A blotchy window looked out onto a one-time industrial section of Kingston, with no activity now but for an occasional police gyrocopter guiding down silently, a sleek bug on an invisible wire. She slammed the door shut. "The more I have to chase you, the harder I'm gonna come down in the end."

He sat across from her, sweat rising. "What about Zachariah Willer? Why didn't you do anything?"

"Before you showed up at his place, he was cooperating."

"What?"

Cape's fingers clomped on a keyboard at her desk. A swarthy, paunchy man in his 30's with

174

stringy black hair, in the form of twittery light, appeared on a raised circle in the floor glowing like a hot plate. Jonathan saw the emblem of the Hudson River Patrol on his gunmetal gray, short-sleeved uniform. "Yeah, I followed her one time," this figure said in a husky voice. "She went to Tristesse."

"Who was she with?" inquired a voice, which was Cape's.

"Some prick with a cap, collar up."

"Who?"

"I tried to see but I couldn't."

"Did you go in?"

"I thought about it. But I was pissed off and fed up... They say - they say once you go in there, you're never the same."

The spectral figure, who was Zachariah Willer - though whom he didn't recall seeing before - disappeared.

Jonathan said, "You arrested him too, then."

"No, I told you, he came in voluntarily."

"Willer never identifies the man she was with. All you see is that he's capable of rage."

"Did you or did you not visit Tristesse with her?"

"I..." He shifted in his seat. "No."

She grinned. "Willer says later that she told him it was the married professor she went in with. She tells him that after she went there."

"She did?" That slipped out. Cape had caught him in the lie. She already knew that he and Mitcha had gone to Tristesse.

"Oh yeah. But she changes her mind about this married guy, the one she's having a thing with. She

175

has a change of heart. She wants to break it off with that one and go back to Willer."

"That's what he would tell you, isn't it? To protect himself."

"Willer says she wanted to have a baby with him."

"Mitcha wanted to have a baby with Willer?" His own voice sounded small to him.

"That's why she wants to get back with him."

That could be a reason for someone else - for Jonathan - to get jealous.

Cape said, "But then - she just... goes away on him. Someone made her go away... You did."

Pain knitted its way through his belly. "But if Willer wanted that - if that's what was happening - you would've heard from him right away. But he never even reported her missing. No one did. You told me that."

"Of course she was reported missing," Cape said. "Zachariah Willer makes a report of the missing girl less than a month after she disappears. Then God-zero comes down. Then everybody knows what time it is - quarter after shit."

His mouth felt so parched, he wanted to ask Cape for water but didn't want to reveal himself in any way.

Cape said, "We also got Quinton Lent. He told us that the bundle, the girl, felt 'in danger' from her boyfriend. This hose who's a married professor."

Quinton might very well have told Cape this; but if Jonathan paid him off, maybe Quinton would recant, maybe that was his plan. "What - what'd he say?"

176

Dr. Rose appeared in the room. "End the conversation with her."

Jonathan said, "What are you doing now?"

"Huh?" Cape said.

She couldn't see Rose. So this ECO had come in by way of the coldcell for only him to view; and this one, with its monochromatic ashen skin, wasn't breathing; no need in this moment for even a semblance of humanity.

"Dr. Rose is communicating with me," he said to Cape.

"You're not obligated to tell her that," the ECO said. "The Canton Police know nothing. Don't tell her anything and don't let her keep baiting you."

"I'm not."

Cape blinked. "What's he saying?"

Rose's ECO said, "Diana and Henry are fine. That's what matters. You shouldn't be here."

Cape flapped her fake hands at him. "Hey, talk to me!"

He spoke to her. "Look, what you've got is lies and hearsay." He tossed out a random possibility. "Not to mention, since you know Mitcha went to Tristesse, God knows what might have happened to her there that has nothing to do with me."

"Maybe she only went there with you."

"No one knows what she was doing in the last few weeks of her life. Plus, you still can't rule out some Martinson connection either, you know that."

"I'll ask you again, what do you know about that?"

"Mitcha was an anonogen. In some part of her, she hated this world. So did Martinson. They did have some kind of relationship."

177

"Martinson was suicidal and also an exhibitionist, like he wanted everyone to share his annihilation. Does that fit a pattern to you of someone who wants to get away with murder? A cold-blooded survivor?"

"Well why was Mitcha's house burned down, after her body was thrown in the river?"

"Why?"

"Because she wasn't killed there but there was still something incriminating."

"That's possible."

"Yes. But Martinson's DNA in the house, at that time, wouldn't really have meant anything, they were working together on a lab project - neither would Quinton Lent's, who lived there on and off, or Willer, the boyfriend. But someone else's might have. Someone who had no reason to be there. Who shouldn't have been in that house!"

"You."

He shook his head repeatedly. "No, no! That's not what I mean, I'm talking about a different person. Someone who also worked with Martinson and got close to Mitcha, too, but was keeping their identity secret. And - by the way! - who might be planning something else right now."

"Quite the assumption," she said.

"You know goddamn well if they could kill three hundred thousand people they would've killed three million if they could."

Cape tucked in between her fingers like she was wearing gloves and her back straightened. "Well, that's some thinking there, Professor. Except Martinson fried himself. And there's no slime trail we can see from him to the girl.

Meantime, Willer and Lent come forward and you don't."

"I told you everything I could."

"No, you pretend you don't know her to me after her year-old leftovers show up in the river."

"I can't believe anyone talks like you."

Rose's ECO said to him, "Get out of here now."

"Here's what I think," Cape said. "I think you and Rose are in this together. You killed Mitcha Ebrey. Now it's a conspiracy between the two of you to cover it up."

"You're out of your mind."

She practically leaped out of her chair. "At least I got a completely human one, scumbag. Somebody's gotta fight you, what you are, you and Rose. Cops do mean something!"

"Stop, I'm sorry, I'm not trying to -"

"If you break the rules of house arrest," she interrupted him, "if you do anything - I swear to you, I will find you wherever you are and kill you myself. I can do that."

He stood dumbfounded - before striding out of Cape's office. He anticipated she might come charging down the hall after him or that he'd be held back at the door to the station house. But he was able to walk out undeterred. This time.

CHAPTER 29

He summoned his car by phone as he waited outside in the cold. The penalty for murder was a cheap Canton execution, done through induced brain anoxia, or oxygen deprivation. Then afterward all body parts could be harvested at will - though his case was original in this regard. What an ironic fate! Within his Ford Roguebat, he called out to Dr. Rose, that invisible but ubiquitous presence; the fat spider spinning a web that still held him in sticky check. "Cape assumes you know something and that you're just protecting me, no matter what. You heard her, she thinks that somehow we're in this together."

"What's your question?"

"Well. Are we?"

"Your reputation as a scientist and professor, a husband and father, will remain intact."

"Can't you give me a straight answer?"

"I've just given it to you."

"No, you haven't!"

"I asked you before not to challenge me. That's for your own good."

"You heard. Mitcha's murder and the arson fire at her house could've been separate, the second crime designed to cover up the first. But committed by different people. I do think Cape's willing to believe that too. That alone means there could have been a conspiracy. A conspiracy of some kind."

"You know everything you need to and Janice Cape knows nothing."

"No! I still don't know exactly what happened to me in my lab. Something that should never have happened. Then - everything that was done to me afterwards - by you. Because you're keeping it secret - the Lazarus Experiment, huh? You're inside my own brain, whether I like it or not, which I don't... Also, I still don't know why I had that horrible vision of Henry - even if that's not your fault. That particular vision!... I don't even understand why I can't remember everything that went on between me and the girl." Night fog flew past his car windows in plumes as he drove off. Minutes passed. "Nobody told me Henry was going to a special school, what about that? What else don't I know that I should?"

"For him, it's not a special school, it's a normal school."

"OK, OK..." These sounded like programmed responses, now – maybe earlier they were too. Venting his searing aggravation would resolve nothing. "I want to thank you for taking my family to safety but I do need them."

"Diana and Henry are sleeping soundly," the voice in his head said. "I will let you make contact soon."

"I want to talk to Diana."

Dead air. He cursed softly.

He cruised to a promontory on the Hudson, the past few days roiling within his mind, waiting in vain for memories to boil over. A prism effect of moonlight and city light spread a purple welt along the low mountains. Trying to piece together what he did remember, he ruminated on what it meant to Mitcha that she was an anonogen. She was self-

181

destructive and outwardly destructive. She'd brought him to the abandoned laboratory of Jefferson Clark to give him a clue about herself; the place where she was raised, orphaned and isolated, a target of behaviorist experiments gone awry. Clark, disgraced, had died a natural death a decade ago, but he still had his teeth fastened on Mitcha's bones, by her own reckoning. This appeared to be what she was implying to him, that first night they spent together, in the college pub, when she told him, "You don't know me."

Where did love into enter into it? He felt sorry for Mitcha even now but he couldn't say he ever loved her. He had wanted to possess her like Zachariah. That was a mistake. He'd been a fool to jeopardize his life with Diana. Real love was what he'd had with her. Stability, comfort, tenderness, even if passion had dissipated between them, that was what mattered and he and Diana knew it. They'd both made equally culpable mistakes and come back to that truth.

Meantime, there had been someone who heard who went in and out of Mitcha's home, whether it was Jonathan, Zachariah Willer, James Martinson, or the elusive someone else. It was the person who'd hidden upstairs. Quinton Lent.

Someone who might still give him information. About something. Or who might reveal himself in a different way.

In the car, Jonathan called him and got no answer. Through the number, he could pinpoint the location of that phone. So he sped off towards Quinton's location, woods around him shadowy and silent, and feeling for some reason that he was racing to avoid another catastrophe.

Along the east bank of the Hudson, at a gravelly cul de sac that was a long-ago train station, a makeshift docking facility had been shored up. It was where Quinton Lent's signal was taking him. Jonathan parked, observing that the broken pier compelled a motley group towards it, barely identifiable since the streetlights were smashed. A ferry appeared, some century-old party boat, its pale wood turned rumpled as hard cheese. He mixed in with the mongrel rest, clambering aboard the vessel in the clapping tide, which chugged forward through the soupy eddies of the Hudson. Even up close it was hard to tell if the people around him were men or women, heads down, shoulders arched, some eyes so sunken in they looked gouged, some near collapse and only upright because the crowd pressed in on them. Occasionally, the full moon lit one of the faces onboard to reveal a scar, a stalactite tooth or a blue tattoo. The boat maneuvered in smoky quiet then didn't dock so much as bang into another pier. Someone with waxy turtle-green hair threw up overboard.

So they made it to an island, a useless quarter mile slab in the middle of the Hudson, where a compact, abandoned stone fortress sat, dating back centuries. The group marched as one in darkness. He found a combination homeless encampment and old-time "shooting gallery." Inside the concrete edifice, folding tables were set up in an atrium like at a bazaar offering syringes, pill bottles, octopus masks that penetrated every orifice in the head, genital catheters, even a suicide soup. No electricity was available. Stick-figures probed and plucked, scurrying in the rust-colored light of oil lamps. This island was cut off even as it was monitored - the modern equivalent of a leper colony. He jostled through this crowd and kept a lookout for Quinton's purple coat and dreadlocks.

He didn't expect to hear somebody preaching, speaking through a laryngeal voice-box in a monotone. He wore a black coat and porkpie hat. "My brothers and sisters, in 5,000 million years the sun will start to run out of hydrogen. It will grow brighter and hotter but its gravitational field will loosen so the orbit of Earth will widen outward. Our planet will grow colder. It will enter a new ice age. But after that, the sun will grow to be a red giant. So big that it will swallow the Earth and inner planets. All the planets will be incinerated as they're absorbed in its ultra-hot layers. Brothers and sisters, before this comes to pass, comes the Transformation."

He lost the sound of this idiot's voice as it cracked, without amplification in the ambient rustle and hiss. He seemed to be proffering that as the body and mind revert to a kind of infantilism in old age, so would the race revert. Jonathan watched how the space around this man took on a steely glow like a ten foot pond suspended in mid-air in a wan holographic projection. Suddenly peering out through this phony pool were seal-like figures, slit-eyed, but with both flippers and hands and the fleshy faces of humans. This was the destination of the human race in old age, the man in the porkpie hat said. In the final days allotted to the planet by the sun, human beings will re-submerge in the sea

184

from whence they came billions of years before. Risen from the sea, and to return to the sea. There was no salvation in technology, only the natural will of the planet. The exhortation to a natural death.

He caught sight of Quinton Lent shuffling away from this demonstration slump-shouldered, looking affected by it.

"Hey, Quinton!" he called out.

Quinton turned around and froze in place, unsure how to react. His face even looked bigger, red as the inside of a watermelon and swelled. Drugs were physically distorting him. "Like, what …" He started pulling at his hair.

He grabbed Quinton's shoulders. "Just tell me anything you think you know. I'll pay you, I will!... I'm sorry about Mitcha, I know about her past, I realize she was a sad and vulnerable girl. She needed help and no matter what, I didn't help her. Now, just help me save my family, please."

He waited as Quinton glanced around, steadying himself in place, suddenly seeming more alert. "Let's take in the outdoors," Quinton said.

He led Jonathan to a point outside where the river swirled around them, frothing on the stony shoreline. He held his hand out. Jonathan shoved a bunch of bills into it. Quinton said, "This? Bullshit. I lick your asshole, you lick mine."

He punched more money into his hand and said, "That's what I got right now. I can get more. What did you mean by that note you left me? 'Who you really are will infect you?' Start there, can you?"

Quinton gave a stupid grin. "Why don't you talk to that doctor of yours?"

185

"Why would you say that? You don't know anything about Dr. Rose."

"That time you collared me wasn't the only time."

"The only time what?"

"Let's say I got an idea of stuff that's goin' down. Didn't you fuckin' process that?"

"You were spying on us more than once!"

Quinton looked off into a curlicue of scarlet moonlight on the filthy water. "Maybe... I know about your kid."

"What! What about Henry? You know I had some kind of a - a vision, or whatever it was, about him? Is that what you mean?"

"Yeah, a vision." He seemed to be scoffing at it. "I know you would miss him if he was gone."

"How dare you -"

Quinton began walking away from him. "Don't you set foot here again. I find you, you don't find me."

He caught up to Quinton. "No! Talk to me!"

Quinton sneered and raised a fist. Acting on impulse, Jonathan swung and connected with his bony cheek first. "Don't go near my family, I told you!"

The bent, little man made a low noise in the back of his throat and crimped at the waist. Then he slid a hunting knife from a sheath under his pant leg. "Fall back, cock-sucker!"

Jonathan had to catch his breath, his heart beating too fast, head throbbing. But he didn't want it to go this way. He wasn't done with Quinton. He sputtered out another of the questions that brought him here. "Is it true she wanted to have a baby?"

In a second, Quinton said, "Hah. Yeah. I guess she wanted to have a baby."

"So she did. With Willer."

"Not with Willer... With you!"

Jonathan stepped closer, mouth open, unable to speak.

"Tomorrow at midnight," Quinton said. "Be home. You pay me more and I tell you more."

Quinton stalked away. Jonathan hurried after him over the rocky ground. "Wait!"

"Tomorrow at midnight." Quinton did an about face and lunged - poking him in the neck with what felt like a pin. Then Quinton jumped back and chortled. Jonathan could barely move for a second then he felt on the deck of a thrashing ship as he tried to step forward. Dryness clawed at his throat. "What..?"

"A little acceleron, won't last long. A freebie. No worries, brokedown man."

Jonathan lost him to the darkness. Metal blades whirled in the distance and a tiny shape of red and white light approached through the night mist. He didn't know if this belonged to the Canton police or to the Bluestone Clinic, both hell-bent to claim him for different reasons. He didn't want to wait to find out but he couldn't run. He felt dizzy and unsupported by his legs, with no center of gravity, and fell. He tried to drag himself forward. Then sound seemed a muddy growl before his ear smacked raw earth.

"What'd I do," he mumbled to nobody.

With eyes closed, a vision of a viral worm conjured itself. In some writhing, new inside ecosystem, he caught sight of a silky eye, lidless, swiftly retreating into the depths of this non-place. He chased the comet tail of this demi-worm to plunge into embedded memory -

He stands with Mitcha in an unused office off the main weather lab. There are no windows but a fake sky duplicates the passage of day and night, azure sifting into brandy-amber with an onion- full moon. They've come here before, almost no one else does.

He isn't sure he hears her right at this time, that she would say what she did.

I don't want to wait. You should know, she tells him.

He looks at her but his eyes must have reflected a watery panic rather than lust.

I want you, he says.

I want you too. That's not enough anymore.

She withdraws the wafer-thin taser from the pocket of her jeans. She runs the injector down his chest and jabs him through his shirt; and with the blistering jolt, heat and pressure well inside him. She draws back from him, bruises blooming on her upper arms. Bruises not from Zachariah Willer or anyone else but from him.

In this incongruous context, she repeats what she's said: I want to have a baby.

She wants to have a child now and is prepared to do it.

To breed is to survive.

In her mind, it's all making sense. No more anonogens. She has to right the wrong of what was done to her. She believes in natural childbirth. She believes a woman should keep her child; should know who her child is; should not let science intrude. Even if she's gone about things the wrong way in the past, this is the right way, she thinks now, to find a man who will provide what she wants.

But why him? He has a son to care for already and a marriage he will protect.

They have been brought together as lovers for a reason, she says. He is the one for her. She knows he is a good father. What is between them will supersede everything.

But he can't tell her that he will do this.

If you don't, I'll leave you, she tells him.

He still can't say it.

What about it? she says

A charge runs through his body now, desire uncoiling from its hidden places, ripping at him from within -

All right, he tells her, I will.

You promise, she asks.

I promise.

CHAPTER 30

He lay clutching at dirt as the flashback vanished abruptly. Minutes after he collapsed, so did the effect of whatever he was injected with. He looked back into Quinton's drug lair with its distant clamor and what looked like broken, blinking chains of torchlight. No one waiting for him on the ground or in the sky.

How had he remembered without the mind-d! It could have been Quinton's drug that pushed him into another consciousness. The mind-d, his own creation, motivated neurons of his brain to start communicating with each other and the extra push helped.

Maybe it was even a form of his memory rebooting, without Dr. Rose's help.

He started running.

He agreed to have a baby with Mitcha.

It would be a natural child like his own son, whom she coveted, he thought.

He'd been out of his own head, in that moment. He wiped away useless tears - tears for her, for Diana, for himself. Did Mitcha get pregnant? There might not have been enough time for her to even check before she was killed. So no one would have known.

He wanted to assume he never fulfilled his disgraceful promise to her.

He made it safely off the island. He stumbled from the ferry in the shadows, back to his car.

Quinton wasn't bluffing about Mitcha wanting to have a baby with him. Quinton had information that could implicate him further in her murder, he was sure of it. He would have to keep the rendezvous and pay him.

What had he done!

He thought about Quinton being armed with a hunting knife. It wasn't just Zachariah Willer who kept weapons. Mitcha had been cut up with a knife and in his wretched waking nightmare, so was Henry. Now, Quinton had just made a veiled threat against Henry. So was that vision of his son telling him anything? There did seem a possible sense to it, now - the jagged sense of prophetic dreams.

Last year, Quinton himself might have threatened Mitcha for money and he wound up stabbing her to death over it. Then all this obfuscation and game playing by Quinton was just to protect himself.

"Doctor," he called out to Rose breathlessly within the car interior. "You stored my 'dream' of Henry?"

It took a second for the once more audio-only response. "That data is available."

"Give it back to me please."

"Why?"

"Can't you just do it! I don't know, there might be something else there, some sign I missed…"

He heard a quick chirping sound inexplicably from somewhere in the invisible machinery within him. He pulled the car over and stepped out into the cold night air. A filmy globe appeared to grow out of this sterile earth.

191

He stepped through the sphere, feeling nothing by doing this, gasping to find himself back in his little boy's room, though in a fluttery near-translucence, as he relived this scene through the coldcell. Henry sprawled out bloody in bed, looking deformed on a soaked sheet. Jonathan snapped his head away from this gruesome sight and jumped out of the seeming bubble. Rose had let him re-experience this and it only made him sicker and more confused. "All right. Thank you for doing that. But I didn't - couldn't... figure out anything else."

The bubble went away and he blinked rapidly on the dark road. He was literally grasping at air. He was feeling as though he was being spun in circles by all the different forces around him. But he was doing it to himself.

In the car, he sent Janice Cape a message: "Look, this addict, Quinton Lent, carries a hunting knife in a sheath underneath his pant leg. Maybe you already checked to see if it could be the murder weapon - but just in case you didn't know about it..."

He hung up and yelled out to Rose, "Where are my wife and son? You promised me."

In a minute, Diana's face flickered on the screen in its fuzzy three-d. "'Lo," she said, which sounded like a moan. She lay in a bedroom not their own, wearing a rumpled tangerine nightgown and clutching a pillow.

"Diana. Everything all right? You OK? Henry?"

"Yeah. Where are you?"

"Just came from talking to that woman, you know, Detective Janice Cape. The police still don't know anything."

"Why would Dr. Rose allow that?"

"He didn't. He had nothing to do with it and he tried to stop it. How's Henry doing?"

"What'd she have to say, that cop?"

"Just more questions. You know. I told you, they don't know anything. Can I talk to Henry?"

"Still sleeping."

"Well, all right."

"I'll get him."

"No, don't bother to wake him... He's good?"

"Yes," she said in a second.

"Where are you?"

"I can't tell you exactly."

"Why?"

"Because... I don't know. Private compound. Empty. Big. The only ones here."

"So, how is it?"

"Peaceful enough."

"Uh huh. Good. So - see you guys soon?"

"I don't know."

"Diana?"

"Yeah?"

"Henry's OK, right?"

"What're you inquiring, my love?"

She turned her face from the phone screen and he saw only strangely bent waves of hair. He sensed she'd ingested a lot of something, presumably Eufonia. "I know he's been through... so much."

"Well..."

193

"I know he's going to classes at the clinic. I think that's good."

"Jon," she said. It sounded like a moan. She left the sentence unfinished.

"You want to say something?"

"You're gonna meet that little shit, that Quinton Lent again, aren't you? You want to."

"What? I..." Dr. Rose could know this because he could pick up on all Jonathan's interactions. "Why would Rose tell you that?"

"He wants me to try to talk you out of keeping another meeting with that guy."

"Well... Look, I keep telling you, the more that I know the more I can defend myself. This guy may be behind things in even more ways than we know." He wouldn't go deeper into his last encounter with Lent. "Diana. Listen. I know I should never have gotten involved with her. I am sorry."

"Well... All right, there's something else you need to know. Something I've got to tell you."

"What?" On the car screen, her head was hidden from him by the pillow. "Diana?"

"It's about Dr. Rose."

"What about him?"

"He -"

Her image on the screen disappeared with a silent pop. "Diana!"

His mind went momentarily blank.

"Rose, what the hell are you doing? Did you cut her off?... Goddamn it! Bring her back."

Nothing. "They better be OK. What -?"

Trying to imagine what Diana might have been trying to say that Rose wouldn't allow, he couldn't finish.

194

He drove to his campus as fast as the car would take him.

CHAPTER 31

Within the university library, he found an empty cubicle. He lowered the opaque glass dome hinged on the side of a plastic desk, sealing himself in. He felt his breath blow back at him in this abalone-hued shell, smelling of sweat, sweet colas and body odors. A pump banged into gear and cold air hissed in as a vast mirrored structure loomed. He advanced up a hard-angled glacial wall, feeling a slight vertigo.

"Look up Dr. Oskar Rose." His pod gave the effect of zooming ahead. There had to be some place to start. "What's the Lazarus Experiment?"

Weightless logs of light fell around him, milk-white and violet. The program wouldn't acknowledge that question. "Anything about his work at the Bluestone Clinic."

A non-descript female voice said, "Dr. Rose's work has advanced into the private sector. Confidential under Canton law."

"I want to cross-reference Dr. Rose with Dr. Jonathan Kelton."

"No information available."

No, why should there be? Everything that happened to Jonathan at the Bluestone Clinic was secret anyway.

"I want to cross-reference Dr. Rose with Quinton Lent." Why would Rose be talking to Diana about Quinton?

"No information available."

196

But it seemed now there was some kind of interrelationship.

And it was possible Quinton was guilty of murder.

What was Rose up to? "What's Dr. Rose doing at Tristesse?"

"No information available."

"Then… what the hell - cross reference Dr. Rose with James Martinson."

"All information has been uploaded to authorities."

That told him nothing but he'd be hard-pressed to make a connection between Martinson and Rose. He already found out Martinson had never been Rose's student. And if there was a living Martinson co-conspirator at the university, he had no name to go with it.

He couldn't imagine what Diane wanted to tell him. He said, "Look, I just want to know more about Dr. Rose."

Rose's bio took shape. He was born in 2031, ten years before Jonathan, in Geneva. Apparently, his father Rainer was a billionaire pharmaceuticals executive. The inheritance had a hand in Rose's being able to open his own clinic. His mother was Genevieve Dussault, a little-known Swiss actress. An inordinately long list of the schools he attended appeared in text. Young Oskar Rose had gone from boarding school to boarding school before landing at Cambridge at age 16 and then Princeton. Jonathan got the gist that the boy genius was a temperamental prodigy with demanding yet determinedly aloof parents.

Then he hit a wall of news. "On October 3, 2051, at 5:45 PM, at the Grand Forum Hotel in Rome, Dr. Rainer Rose, born Rainer Klaus Rosengren in Berlin, is led out in handcuffs to an awaiting motorcade of carabinieri instead of his usual limousine."

The doctor's father, Rainer, was accused of killing Rose's mother Genevieve. At the best hotel in the city, he threw her off the balcony.

Rainer was arrested for the murder but never convicted. Genevieve had been drunk and full of painkillers and his whereabouts within their penthouse suite were not provable. She could have fallen by accident. Rainer went into seclusion after this and continued working in private, though under a cloud.

Dr. Rose's father murdered his mother.

"Christ," he mumbled. "Look, there must be something else here about Dr. Rose's work. He conducted research in this university, there's got to be something."

The covers of three short volumes then appeared in front of him wan as lima beans. The titles he read were "Schematic of the Past," "The Biological Cast of Past, Present and Future" and "Targeted Psychogens." Rose burst to life in mid-lecture on a small three-d loop lecturing in a classroom. "This, my friends, is the journey of the future - not out into empty and impossible distances but into our own minds. To slit open the very envelope of reality to see what's inside…" Behind him were equations on a blackboard, with a heading referencing a Dali painting: "The Persistence of Memory."

He shut it off. He suddenly realized how shamefully myopic his reliance on his previous logic had been. He said, "I want to cross-reference Dr. Rose with Mitcha Ebrey."

Why hadn't he considered this before!

A three-year old class roster materialized.

Mitcha had been Dr. Rose's student.

He said, "You son of a bitch."

What he had also just been able to find out so easily was that Rose's experiments here at the university involved memory control.

He no longer had to ask himself why he couldn't remember things that were so crucial, and why his explosive flashbacks cut themselves off. It seemed as if something had been blocking his memories all along. But it wasn't residual trauma or an inadvertent side effect of the coldcell. It was purposeful: his memory had been controlled by Dr. Rose from the start, beyond the power of the mind-d to work. It was as if Jonathan kept getting knocked off-line.

Even as far as the mishap in his lab, he thought, Rose would most likely have known what substances were present that nearly destroyed him. The doctor was never anything but evasive about it.

When taken in combination with Rose's experiments in thought control, it seemed...

Jonathan was being set up.

The doctor knew Mitcha - so, what if he knew her intimately?

What if he went to Tristesse with her too?

What if he killed her there?

199

Maybe it was by mistake. Anything at Tristesse could have gotten out of control. Now, Rose had taken control of Tristesse.

That meant the Lazarus Experiment was not just about its purported breakthrough, organic reconstruction with a coldcell symbiote.

It was about getting away with murder.

Like Rose's own father.

The library pod got flipped up from the outside. Two men stood there in white, full-body gear. They were from the Bluestone Clinic. He couldn't see their faces, as one gripped him tightly by the back of the neck. Jonathan grunted as one man raised what resembled a drill, an almost invisibly thin electrode emerging. He inserted this into Jonathan's brain.

CHAPTER 32

He soared back to consciousness after being knocked out cold. He found he was flying in a hovercraft. He peered through a porthole and saw the vehicle veer toward the entrance to Rose's annex at the Bluestone Clinic. It looked like a Pharaoh's tomb, above him a five-story tall archway supported by two behemoth pillars, blank-faced, male and female stone idols.

He passed out again.

He came to, still in flight though he was indoors. He didn't know how much time had passed or where he was but he was looking at a bronze-colored tank about ten feet high, a huge steel circle with extended pylons, which radiated outward like a primitive pictograph of the sun. At their tips were what looked like classroom desks with unmanned medical monitors. It was no longer human hands that performed complicated surgery, which is what he figured was happening. He sat in a chair that was rising, ascending on a crane, edging over the tank now aglow with a sea green, aquarium light. A pitch-colored, snowman shape in the water, like a startling image of death, a floater, a drowning victim.

A sub-sea pinging rang through his skull. A robotic arm fixed a skullcap on him, a tinny crown of micro-thorns he could barely feel. He was lowered in a hammock-like harness. Pulsating wet walls swallowed him like a snake would a mouse, a hot, toothless, numbing inhalation.

Submerged, wrapped in what seemed like chainmail, he could breathe normally but remained deaf and blind in the aquatic chamber. In this darkness and silence, he experienced the taste of fire, not smoke but as if fire had a taste and every inch of his skin, taking it in tiny, loose-fingered flames, swallowed it. Another image took hold, as tingling spread: that of a million arachnids digging minute pincers into his flesh. But they could spin silk from their jaws, unfurling through him.

There was no pain. There was oddly a sense of release. It seemed his body effortlessly turned skinless. He couldn't help but imagine an exquisite night bloom, which no one could see, while his own blood opened to airy pockets around him...

Days might've passed before he was startled awake by the feel of his own body again. He lay in bed, the ceiling above a serene white arc.

The drama of that synesthesiac transfiguration lingered in his mind. He'd undergone an operation in the sensory deprivation tank, in an ideal state of weightlessness, he could deduce that.

Why? Because he'd learned too much? What had been done to him by Rose now?

He raised his head to look down at his bare arms and the concavity of his chest under a hospital gown. His skin was an almost phosphorescent quartz-red. He said, "Where are my wife and son?"

"Everything is as it was." Rose's voice.

"How long have I been here?"

"Two days."

So of course, he'd missed the meeting with Quinton Lent, as Rose and Diana wanted. "Am I your prisoner now?"

202

Straps of silver energy held his wrists and ankles firmly but lightly. He still wore the bracelet that represented his state of detention by the police. Not even Rose could get rid of that, after all.

He tried to sit up but was too weak. A fluid whiteness played over him, around him. He called out Rose's name several times then murmured "Diana" and "Henry" over and over, until he drifted back to sleep.

It was another amorphous hyphen of time before Rose returned, wearing his lab coat and running a hand over his shiny bald head. The glowing white room, unchanged otherwise, seemed to pulse in tandem with the beating of Jonathan's heart.

"You've emerged revitalized," the doctor said. "After tearing around stupidly."

"You could've stopped me any time you wanted," Jonathan snapped.

"I was trying to influence your actions, not control them. I told you before, I didn't think you were doing harm in the beginning and it was crucial that you felt you had free will."

"So why'd you stop me now?" Jonathan sat up in bed. "You knew Mitcha Ebrey, didn't you, doctor?"

Rose looked away moodily into the opaque whiteness. "You have to disconnect that line of thought."

"Your father killed your mother, I know that."

Rose looked quizzical. "What are you saying, Jonathan?"

"Do you think we're all goddamn blind?"

"No, in fact everything is in plain sight. That's old news that dogged me for part of my professional life."

"So what do you have to say for yourself?"

"I never believed my father did it. He was distraught afterward. I loved my mother. I believe so did he, in his way. She had issues of her own that had nothing to do with him. And this has nothing to do with anything."

"I don't think they loved each other or they loved you."

"Be that as it may. I don't know why you're bringing it up."

"Because you're not who you pretend to be. Like your damn father."

"And this means what to you?"

"Janice Cape thinks I killed Mitcha."

"So what do you remember at this point?"

"I know there was violence between us. Me and Mitcha. There was rough sex, drugs - it got out of hand. At Tristesse... But she wanted something else too. She wanted to have a baby with me."

"So what happened?"

Jonathan's brain spun out. "I don't know, I don't know!"

"You're telling me that you still don't know whether you killed her or not?"

"You already know that. You made me forget! That's what I realize now."

"I have only been trying to protect you," Rose said.

"No, protect yourself! I also found out you knew my former boss Jared Wright."

"So? Years ago, I'd wanted to speak to you about your work and I contacted him. We'd gone to Princeton together. I was interested in your practical chemical applications of sanguivent as a blood substitute. A possible key to immortality or at least thousands of years of life."

"So I happened to have a hook-up to the Wright Group while the two of you were in contact," Jonathan said. "When the explosion happened, you already had an ongoing interface with Wright, isn't that true? It must be. Even though I didn't realize it, you knew what was going on in my lab. That's why your people could get to the scene right away, before anyone else. They could act as policemen and fire fighters. By the time the real police got there, your people were done. Fire out, mess cleaned up, taking me with them."

"Yes."

"You didn't plan on it but I did remember what went on at Tristesse. It became the place to go for twisted little sex games... I think, now..."

"What do you think, Jonathan?"

"That you were one of the people who went there."

Rose sighed as if contending with a babbling child.

"Nobody knows anything about your private life. You have no family. Mitcha got to you just like she got to me, right? It wasn't just me and Zachariah Willer...You were her lover, too. Or wanted to be."

Rose didn't respond.

"You probably killed her at Tristesse. Maybe you didn't mean for it to happen or maybe you did.

205

But you covered it up by sealing off Tristesse - after you got rid of the body. Meantime, it was easy to burn down her house to get rid of any trace of your presence there. After that, you wrecked my memory, destroyed any connections I might make between the two of you. I was available as a patsy and a guinea pig, both! A lucky coincidence for you. An amazing one! You saved my life but you got a coldcell variant to eat a piece of my mind. That allowed you to shield yourself behind Canton law. Isn't that it!"

Jonathan heard a dense squeaking and turned as a wooden door, blackened by fire and pitted, swayed open. He was imagining it: he knew it was being imagined for him through the coldcell. He rose from the bed and seemed to inch his way through this phantom door into a cavernous church interior. Dead bats had become bloody peat thickening, dripping on rafters. In his mind, as seen through his ocular implants as an eclipse of true reality, he plodded barefoot down an ethereal aisle that led to an alabaster altar. As he moved forward, he kicked aside quasi-holographic entrails, remnants of animal sacrifices, maybe crypto-pagan, Santeria, retro-Judeo-Christian. He raised his eyes to the twisted, blood-spattered crucifix. A figure outstretched its arms towards the vaulted ceiling with its frescoes blotted by smoke damage. It was Rose. His eyes, orange-rimmed, met Jonathan's. Rose wanted him to experience this. "So?" Jonathan said. "So what?"

"So you see how Tristesse looked once," Rose finally spoke. "Does it help you remember anything more?"

"No."

Tristesse dematerialized.

"I visited the church for the first time right after God-zero. I just fed you an image of that. I can't do anything more about your remembering."

"Bullshit. What am I doing back here in your clinic? What the hell are you doing to me now!"

"There has been a reason for everything."

"I told you, I know the reason. You killed Mitcha Ebrey and you wanted me to take the blame."

"No," Rose said heavily. "This is the reason."

CHAPTER 33

The doctor crooked a finger and the wall in front of them opened. A barren, dimly lit basement hallway stretched in front of them. It was real. "Come," Rose said.

They walked to the first and only door, solid metal. It opened. Jonathan followed him into what seemed a combination of cave and freezer, bright as ice, with hanging meat shiny as new bricks. It appeared there were whole carcasses rotating slowly, suspended not on hooks but threads of light.

Rose waved him forward. Jonathan maneuvered through an aisle of flesh but it wasn't actual flesh. He saw a white rat dangling in mid-air, blank-eyed, veined black like an uncleaned shrimp; then a dove like some macabre bone china ornament; then, stunningly, a huge orangutan, with fur dark as coffee grounds. It had a small, perfectly round projectile hole through its head. It seemed to stare at Jonathan and give him a toothy smile.

"The simulacrum," Rose pronounced.

"A place of likenesses? Just ECO's. Copies of ECO's? So what?"

"Harbingers of something much greater."

"What the hell does that mean?"

"Subject data."

"So these poor animals were guinea pigs of some kind too. For what!"

"These are all final corpora. The orangutan went insane, started beating its head against its cage. It had to be killed. These are destined for removal, they don't really matter, you're right."

Beyond the upside down ape a gray door appeared labeled with a number Jonathan recognized. It was what he'd seen in Stillwell's files.

The Lazarus Experiment.

He tensed deep inside. The door flipped open. He practically reeled at the sight of a little girl, hanging in the air, arms pressed to her sides, wearing only a T-shirt and panties. Her being shimmered the color of steaming rum.

"What is this!"

Rose said, "The girl drowned. She'd been dead too long to be revived."

"I know, images to be replicated, so what the hell are you trying to convince me of?"

A girl walked in through the left wall, the same girl. She wore the same T-shirt and panties. Only instead of the boyish figure of what might have been a 10 year old, she'd begun to flesh out, like a 14 year old, and so looked disturbingly and incongruously sensual, her cheekbones more prominent and her auburn hair several inches longer. "Hi," she said. She was looking at Jonathan but as with any ECO, through him. He looked at Dr. Rose again in puzzlement.

Rose said, "Amelia has grown in real time. And she's learned."

"Do you know what actually happened to you, Dr. Kelton?" the girl asked.

"No."

She recited, "Microscopic chips got implanted throughout your neural net that contain packets of information, as your body was being reconstructed. Your senses had to be rendered inactive within the module so your sensory experiences could be altered in ways that would be undetectable to you. In this way, your sense of reality could be re-created. You know? Or really, you don't know." She giggled.

"Rose, tell me what kind of a show this is!"

The doctor said, "We tried many things, many times. Finally, we got it right. It took a year, Jonathan. You were here in the Bluestone Clinic for a year. We worked on Amelia for years before that. By the time you came along, we were ready. You were right about one thing. Your appearance on the scene was an amazing coincidence."

The doctor made another gesture and it all vanished, the dead animals and the hapless Amelia, apparitions gone back into digital storage.

Rose led him out, until the two men once again stood alone in the bare white room where he'd been lying. "I don't get what she - it - said about my operation," Jonathan said.

"You wanted to know what we found in the wreckage of your lab. You wouldn't stop asking. Well, now I'll show you. I have to. This fool, this worthless interloper, Quinton Lent, has been taken in by the police. You didn't know that but he has. And he's talking."

"Talking? Talking about what!"

"What he found out by spying on you. Did you know he was spying on you?"

"Yeah, he did tell me that. But I didn't know what he found out, or thought he did."

210

"Because of him, because of all of the unforeseen developments, we've had to abort this phase of the experiment... My God, you made things so difficult."

"Me? Look, Diana wanted to tell me something before you cut her off on the phone. About you, about what you were doing. So what'd she want to say?"

"You still don't understand, do you?... I'm sorry."

A sudden mist descended. Words began to form and clarified, an official status file:

Jonathan Kelton, DEAD.

Then another file coalesced in the mist.

Henry David Kelton, DEAD.

CHAPTER 34

"What is that?... That's a lie. Just two days ago - I was with Henry, held him…"

"That's the point - that's what we had to make sure of. And it worked. Your son, Henry, was real to you."

"What happened to him!"

"He's the same as he has been."

"What the hell are you talking about? He's with Diana now. She just told me that. And you said so yourself. They're at your place up north, whatever it is, your compound."

"You did speak to her and you're right, there was something she wanted to tell you."

"So where's Henry?"

"I understand this is difficult."

Jonathan roughly wiped his eyes with the back of a hand. "We sat in the backyard, ate dinner together. I saw him playing in his room. I held him in my arms! He was dirty from his baseball game."

"Yes. But he's not here. Or anywhere."

Rose pointed at the analysis of the fire debris that hung before them now. "Kerosote. The cause of the explosion. You were working with it."

"So I was? And you didn't tell me?"

"Look at the file now. You were both caught in the blast. You could be revivified. Henry couldn't. There just wasn't… enough to work with."

"What…" Flat bio-imaging took shape on the air-screen. He saw his name, then witnessed his own excarnation; a diagram indicated his butchered

212

viscera. He recognized an anchored twig image, central to the diagram, which depicted his vertebral canal. It was knotted uncompromisingly to his brainstem.

Rose continued, "Your cranial cavity was more protected than Henry's. Your isocortex overall OK, corpus callosum not impossibly traumatized…"

"That's what you had to work with, with me?" He echoed Rose's words dizzily.

"It was enough. We found out, that was enough."

A different image replaced his. A smaller figure looking more like newly dug fossil remains, disjointed, once-connected, now-broken lifelines, took shape. "Henry was not so lucky," Rose said.

Tears welled fiercely now. "I just… don't see."

"It was all to help you," Rose said.

"But - but the fire was contained. The house was O.K. Henry must've - he was out!"

As he stood there shaking, he forced himself to reconstruct the moment before the fire. Then another memory struck like a lancet. His mind seemed to rupture and re-form…

Two days after they return from the Adirondacks, Jonathan is in his lab, alone, the steel door flush with ceiling and floor, the firewall. Beyond, Diana has surprised Henry with his favorite, salmon mousse and cold Mexican lime soda, for being such a good boy on the trip. Then, she drives him to school before doing errands of her own. Occasionally, Diana just likes to drive without a destination; a means of getting out of the house, she says, a brief freedom.

So the house sits empty.

213

This is what he thinks as he works.

From across the lab, an eyelet screen wakens to life. It scours the up-to-the minute body of knowledge. It can make analyses based on information in his main system, fetch facts that he might have assumed irrelevant, double check and explore others, reach for some unplanned synergy. But often, the expensive gadget just remains blank and silent, with the blind eye of a scavenger at the bottom of the sea.

Now, something registers on the screen - important data being thrust at him. It could be something he needs to know about what he's doing or conclusions he might have reached mistakenly.

He looks over, alarmed.

In a second, the lab door is being opened...

But who's here - who would come in?

He remains fixed on the door while at the very same time, the small computer flashes an urgent warning behind him -

This memory sheared off too. Why should that keep happening now!

He fell to his hands and knees and threw up, a thin, horribly bitter fluid. What had he become alarmed about! That secondary instrument in his lab had warned him of something. It had turned into a floodlight in the air before him, right before the fire happened.

Could it have been Henry coming into the lab?

On all fours, head hanging down, he asked once more, "Where's Henry?"

"You saw the report," Rose said. "A summation. Look again."

Analyses of the hash of fabric, metal, chemicals, stone and flesh clicked into being again in its stream of ghost-type on the air-screen, Kerosote like a shrill expletive.

Rose helped him to his feet and held him upright. He flung his head back and felt his own teardrops flicker into his mouth, with stringy phlegm.

The doctor said, "The priority was saving whoever could be saved, in that moment, and that was you."

"No! Henry kissed me good-bye. In my bed. The last time I saw him…"

His body gave out again and he toppled into Rose's big arms.

He came to in the white room again, silent as a crypt and vague as a cloud. It undulated hypnotically. He heard the doctor's voice. "Jonathan. This is a taped conversation."

It was Diana's voice: "When I came back, part of our home… was just gone. If you hadn't come to me personally, right away, I don't know what I would've done."

"I understand." Rose's voice.

"I want to thank you. So much. I never had to speak to the police, I never had to speak to anyone. You were right there, in my living room, telling me how everything could be made all right."

"Are you willing to commit fully?"

"I think so."

"It will mean watching over your husband closely. He will believe Henry is there. He will see Henry talking to you. But you will not see Henry directly. You'll have to check the monitor to establish the logistics, which you will not be able to dictate, only suggest to Jonathan. You can call up Henry on the screen. Jonathan won't know that you have the cochlear transducer and it will tell you exactly what he hears. Don't be surprised if Henry calls to him from another room suddenly. Jonathan won't know it himself but if he subliminally desires Henry's presence, the boy will stir. Do you understand all this?"

"I don't know..."

"No. Soon enough, it will be commonplace."

Diana said, "I don't even understand everything that happened, I still don't... how my son could have died."

"Now, you won't have to think about it."

Silence. Then the doctor said, "Jonathan, that was recorded two days after the fire in your laboratory."

"You're fooling me," he muttered, still drowsy. "Aren't you?"

"I told you, we didn't even know in the very beginning if we could restore you to full consciousness. You were clinically dead too. In fact, though, your own cortical plasticity, in your condition, made you a very workable subject. The coldcell and the implants took root quickly."

"I still don't believe you about Henry. But God help you, if you're right..."

"What?"

"I'll kill you."

Despite the words, his emotions were muted. He didn't move, as though floating within water again, weightless and encumbered at the same time,

216

or like he was hanging in emulsion. Somehow, the white room soothed him, fed him.

The room grew colder, and he pulled the blanket around him like an infirm old man. He shut his eyes.

"I didn't understand everything that happened then... how my son could have died..." Diana's voice, echoing in his consciousness.

Before long, he opened his eyes to find Rose standing by his bed and staring at him. "Diana took pains to see that Henry was memorialized, in her own way."

This time, the words cut into him like a scalpel. His body flooded with heat as if veins opened and gushed within. Tears forced their way out once more. It was all true. Somehow, at this point, he knew it was true. "While I lay comatose? No - unfinished..." He let out a joyless laugh. "Something that could never be finished properly?" Whatever had occurred, now he felt impelled only to lay blame. "How could the fire start!"

"You still can't remember that?"

"Are you still blocking my memories?"

"No. As I've just explained, what I know is that, as soon as the Wright Group interface alerted us, you could be saved, Jonathan. And your son - your son was re-created for you and Diana."

He realized then that it wasn't he himself who represented the Lazarus Experiment.

It was Henry.

CHAPTER 35

"You could think of it as an ECO-Nine." Rose named it.

"But… how could you do that to me?" The doctor sighed heavily once more, as Jonathan drew himself up in bed to face him. "Tell me!"

"I suppose… James Martinson."

"Martinson? What are you saying? What? I'm asking you about my son!"

Rose said, "I'm telling you about the time after your accident."

"You're saying Martinson was involved? What is it? That he killed Mitcha, after all? Do you know that?"

"No. What I'm saying is that because of him, because of what he did, everything got rushed ahead. Can you imagine, a killer on that scale coming out of the very institution - our university - which was designed as a beneficent scientific research facility. That it could give rise to some nihilist rebel who lusted after nothing but mass death. Board members were beside themselves to move ahead. I got complete Canton approval. The Lazarus Experiment overrode everything. Three hundred thousand dead in New York State. People were so devastated over the loss of their loved ones, that seemed all that mattered. That was the rationale."

"That was the rationale…"

"Yes. Towards that end, we sealed off Tristesse."

218

"Why?"

"Tristesse had been used as a crematorium after God-zero, as you know. The ash could be excavated and DNA recovered. Quasi-clones, if you will, could be created - electronic rather than organic. From as little as one useful cell, a cosmos of totipotent cells can be ignited, Jonathan, you understand that. The dead of God-zero could be brought back to life! Even if only in the minds of the bereaved. The dead would be alive - like Amelia, like Henry - and they could grow, mature and change like clones. In reality, they represent implanted, motile information. It's software that can merge seamlessly with the human mesh of hardware. So a living person can commune and co-habit with a non-living one - who is really, literally, under his skin."

Jonathan did comprehend this and thought aloud, "But there were... glitches." Like Henry's erratic statements or behavior, even his occasionally glassy eyes, he considered; in a way sometimes like seeing him in a funhouse mirror.

Rose said, "Henry represents only the beginning. The ECO-Nine is a unique symbiosis... It's time to reinvent the world for good."

In a moment, all of this sinking in, he nodded. It came to him that, in time, a couple marooned in their own longitude and latitude of grief and longing would be able to input other things, so a parent could experience a child not like he was but how the person wanted him to be. Humankind would not have to suffer reality but would create it.

Rose declared, "The ultimate and final journey."

It didn't matter, the sadness was overwhelming. Jonathan fell back on the bed arms at his sides. This stark white room could have been a sepulchre and he might as well have been dead himself.

In the recorded conversation he'd heard, Rose also mentioned the six-inch screen to Diana. He assumed when he saw it that it was some kind of a rudimentary, layman's home medical kit as she told him. He realized now what Quinton Lent must have glimpsed through their window, just by chance: Diana and Jonathan talking to Henry, who only appeared on the screen but not in actuality.

What an astonishing mistake, and preventable. It must have been the reason for Quinton's taunting note. Whatever else Quinton was guilty of - or Jonathan himself - that was what Quinton was bargaining to tell him, about the reality of Henry.

Jonathan said, "Not even the cops... nobody else, not Stillwell, knew about - about Henry?"

"We had to know if there were flaws and what they were. See if you would really believe. We had to keep the testing pure in that way."

"You lying bastard," he mumbled.

Still, maybe Jonathan should have anticipated something like this all along, or figured it out, it wouldn't have been that hard; and as Stillwell might have said, he should appreciate it now.

Could he and Diana patch together a life after this, he thought, after all? For her, Eufonia must have fueled innate dissociative tendencies. She'd seemed comfortable in her role as pretender, lying to Jonathan and Cape - and really, even to herself about her son. She'd interacted with the Henry of her monitor screen: the implants in Jonathan's head that transmitted what he saw and heard were what she desired for herself too, Henry's presence. She'd been wilfully inhabiting a parallel universe.

Jonathan said, "In that 'nightmare' about Henry because of the mind-d - I'd already lived through it. I guess I - maybe I grieved in my mind because I did know."

"Your unconscious mind transposed things, images and locations - a transference of what really happened. Probably so. Yes, like in a dream. What you thought you saw in Henry's bedroom - that was the manifestation."

Jonathan sat up in bed again and held his head. He couldn't help but continue to analyze everything that had been so heartbreakingly effective. "Henry - he appeared to move things around too."

"If any object was touching him, or he was touching it, then it was part of the 'reality drop.'"

"'Reality drop?'" More of Rose's new vocabulary. He could guess what it meant and Rose confirmed it.

"Environment templates could be created out of thin air, provided the space remained empty and there was no competition between unreal and real things."

Jonathan could figure that this ECO Nine-Henry wouldn't have been available for greater interplay. That was why he could never have actually watched Henry play on a ball field, interact with other kids who were real, or been able to see Henry order a hamburger at a fast food place. The ECO-Nine at this stage was suited only to Jonathan's own contained and claustrophobic world.

Then, it was up to Dr. Rose to touch up the white spots on nature's canvas. The phony school registration with the Bluestone Clinic was something that had to be layered on.

Rose said, "Jonathan, all the information about your case would have been uploaded. In time, it would have. To the Canton Police. To the media. Within the next six months or so, you were going to be told everything. In a rational and sensitive way - not like this. And in an atmosphere in which we could have negotiated permanency."

"Permanency."

"Yes."

"Anyway, now - you unwired him. It took all that, what I just went through... Did you - did you turn him off?" He panicked, thinking he might beg the doctor for the chance to live that lie again. That irony wasn't lost on him. He'd gone to every length in search of the truth. And now he regretted he did. "I thought that whatever happened to me - whoever I was before - all I ever wanted was..."

"I know."

"The coldcell is gone?"

"No, the coldcell has not been removed. It will continue to check for anomalies."

"I... don't know what to do. What do I do?"

"Go home to Diana... And put away all this nonsense about me and Mitcha Ebrey. Her having once been in my class is irrelevant."

"So who..."

Rose didn't meet his eyes and turned away. The implication was clear – Jonathan had always been, and remained, the prime suspect.

222

It was crucial, he saw now, that he'd been made to forget the moments that led to the explosion that killed Henry. But in the selective memories reprogrammed by Rose, did Mitcha also get washed into oblivion, in some inadvertent runoff?

In his despair, he uttered, "Doctor, I know why you wanted to get rid of my memories of the fire. But why can't I recall anything about that girl, still?"

"I thought you understood."

"No. What?"

"It's what your wife wanted."

"Diana? What do you mean?"

"We both thought it was for the best. Talk to her."

A doorway re-opened in the white room. Rose disappeared down the dark hall, leaving him alone. He was being cast out.

CHAPTER 36

He found his car outside, parked crookedly on the curb by who knows who, left for him in front of the Bluestone Clinic, with no other cars or people in sight, at dusk. He glimpsed in his rearview mirror and saw how sallow he looked, even more cadaverous, wrists skeletal. He'd been used because he could be; expendable from the start. When Rose saved him, he was still-warm matter to be molded without anyone else the wiser. Now, he'd been thrust aside because he no longer seemed viable.

He sat in the car and wept.

He'd lost Henry. Had he and Diana also lost Dr. Rose's protection? "Are you still in my head?" he called out weakly.

There was no response - no voice in his brain.

He couldn't say that he felt physically worse than days ago. He had to assume the coldcell was keeping him functioning properly; and at the same time it would still keep him monitored by the clinic. But there was no more need for interface with Rose or an ECO surrogate. That only made him feel more lonely.

He headed out onto a rain-slick road. The winter sky spread before him like watery red ink, lights of minimal sky-traffic bleeding through icy fog. He gazed out the car window at the snow-frosted pine trees glittering in the moonlight. The trees stood silent and blind to the human world, to the senseless loss of a human soul. His son.

There seemed no meaning anywhere.

In a minute, Diana's face came on the car screen, her face puffy from crying, her hair a mess. She stood in their living room. Dr. Rose had cast her out as well. She'd been sent away by Rose to begin with not to shelter her from the murder investigation but to perpetuate the charade of Henry in the face of so much police invasiveness, he saw; to make sure he stayed fooled.

He didn't know where to start. "How could you do it?" He didn't mean it to be but it came out as an accusation. "I'm out of the clinic. I know everything."

Her glazed eyes swam away from the screen - as if looking for the ever-receding horizon that was Henry. She bunched her bathrobe in front of her. "I was absolutely amazed! To see you, the way you acted... while I watched my screen, the one the doctor gave me - I could see what you were seeing through the coldcell. Henry was, Jonathan. The screen, it was like a camera watching Henry all the time. He did have a separate life."

"Yes." This experiment would hold a special if slightly different meaning for Rose too, with the untimely and ill-explained loss of his own mother, Jonathan had to think that too.

"If it all worked, they would've put the coldcell in my head, too."

So that was her own endgame. He pictured her co-existing with him in the belly of Rose's lie - as it became widespread and the dead of God-zero reawakened as roving ECO-Nines. She hadn't dealt properly with her grief to begin with and Rose, in his wisdom, concocted a monstrous prescription for denial. He wanted Diana to be lucid and self-aware now but a rational woman wouldn't have been able to accept this deception, these theatrics. Hadn't that occurred to Rose?

For now, he said, "That was what you wanted to tell me before - about Henry. You wanted me to know the truth, is that right? Before Rose cut you off, when we were talking in my car."

"I saw it all falling apart. I did want you to hear it from me. Not from somebody like this Quinton Lent. Dr. Rose said you wanted to speak to him. We knew what Lent was going to tell you... But obviously, the doctor didn't want me to tell you either. Not then, anyway. He was just trying to figure out what to do, at that point."

"Diana... I also know you found out about Mitcha Ebrey."

Her body twitched slightly. "You want to talk about that?"

"I regret everything I put you through." He added, "Like you once said to me, I'm not that person anymore... I disown that person, I loathe him."

"I'm not sure I know who that person was either," she said.

"Well, how did you? Find out?"

"How did I find out?... You told me."

Intermittent, pulpy sleet disfigured the car window as the car drove home. "What do you mean?"

"You were gone almost a year, Jon. Think about it. With no time to hide anything - no idea that you even had to so carefully. So you didn't take all that many precautions, like with your car,

226

there was data there. I could figure it out. I could see past phone records, your interaction with this girl. I could get rid of all those."

"But there was still a back-up file in my car, I could still find her house, you didn't get rid of that."

"I believe you wouldn't have known what was there if it wasn't for the damn mind-d. You wouldn't have had any memory of that house."

"You're right," he said.

"Would you dare blame me now? To try to start over?"

"No. I don't blame you... You didn't know - couldn't know - she was dead."

"Of course not."

"You didn't even find out about her - I mean, that I'd been seeing her, until after the fire in my lab, I assume."

"What a moment that was."

"Yeah, you just - walked me through it."

"It doesn't do it justice."

"Anyway, Rose told you that I couldn't be allowed to remember that Henry was in the lab with me - that he'd been there. For the experiment to work, that memory had to be eradicated... So, you told Rose I had an affair, was that it? He could make me forget about Mitcha too?"

"I mentioned to Rose we had problems that year. I would be glad if your memory could somehow be 'rewound,' you know what I mean? I thought I was being silly. But he told me he thought he might actually be able to take away about nine-ten months or so, in the time before your accident. So... you got those memories wiped out, both the good ones and bad ones. He cut across a whole section of time in your mind. He made that available to me, so I took it! Why shouldn't I? He wanted what I did - he wanted us to be a family again!"

"A family again," he repeated sadly.

"I had to forgive - forgive so much… I just wanted to protect us." Her nails, only days ago manicured and with silvery polish, now looked bitten and irregular, in a pizzicato tapping on the coffee table. "That was one of the ways. Dr. Rose was helping us get on with our lives after something - unspeakable!"

"Yes," he agreed meaninglessly. "Can you tell me anything else?"

"What else do you want me to say? Everything - just changed in a flash."

God help him, it did. He said, "Since the fire didn't spread to the house, Henry must have closed the steel firewall behind him. But Diana, what on earth possessed him to march into the lab?" In any case, didn't the fire seem an accident, after all, Jonathan's fault? "Diana. What could I have done?"

"You still can't remember any more?"

"Not everything, no - that part hasn't changed."

"You think I haven't agonized over it myself? I went out for a drive. I was tired. But I couldn't sit still. Working with that thing, you know, my project."

He thought of her blocking out the Gothic church interior in what also still seemed a mind-numbing irony.

She said, "Henry did what he did on his own. The two of you were alone in the house. I got back and... and - Dr. Rose's people were already here."

But what was his secondary lab unit warning him about? How did that relate to the catastrophe in his lab?

Did it?

Diana asked, "Can Dr. Rose keep the police away now?"

"I... don't know."

"So that ugly woman can come back to the door at any time!"

"Diana... Everything probably will... we'll be OK." But if Cape became able to prove that he'd obtained Kerosote, she could go ahead and charge him officially with murder. How could he tell Diana this, after everything? "I loved Henry so much. And I love you." He shut his eyes for a second and perhaps said these words to a woman in a summer outfit pushing a stroller, holding the hand of a little boy in a place that no longer existed.

She said, "Everything was the way it was supposed to be. And now... How can we live?"

She glared at him then walked away from the screen. A pellucid stone anteroom materialized, as if their house grew an extension within itself and she weaved back into her self-made world of the monastic cathedral to do who knew what; lost to him, and as though carried away on the echo of a church bell. Wintry gray light enfolded her. The car screen went dark.

Tears flooded his eyes. He wouldn't let himself believe that he was beyond redemption. He would not, could not, stop grieving for Henry. But he still wanted to know who he'd been, what he'd done. It seemed the only way to save his own soul, whatever that was.

His wipers punched away the tumbling sleet and his car felt drafty and cold though the heat spouted full blast. He shivered. He felt unable to be made well ever again. The last he could recall of solid food was in his kitchen, where he'd seen that Diana had left out peas, desiccated by the time he got to them, while his own synthetic, antibiotic food supplements sat ready for him bagged in plastic and refrigerated separately like medical specimens. But he had no appetite.

The glove compartment of the car popped open. A voice message came in from Dr. Rose, not through the coldcell but his regular car channel. "Jonathan. I've left you with something."

He saw a mind-d sitting in the glove compartment next to the car's mesh-mask and flare gun.

The doctor said, "It's a new one, it's clean, there shouldn't be distortions."

So the doctor was trying to help him. Surprised, disbelieving even, he said barely audibly, "Thank you."

"I..." For the very first time, Rose himself seemed at a loss for words. "Good luck, Jonathan."

He slipped this new mind-d, more compact and dense than his homemade one, behind his ear. He would try again to force the life that he'd once led to compel him - the what-wasn't-there-of-it. If he couldn't come up with more soon, something illuminating, something that could be exculpatory, he would have nothing - no alibi, no excuses; only a guilty past no matter what.

Diana didn't contact him back. Probably, at least at this moment, she didn't want him. So he drove to the college. He parked in front of the Climatology Lab. A miasma-like fog clung to the building as he sat still. He tried to think about time he and Mitcha might have spent together here. No more voices from the coldcell, no noises from outside.

He'd done wrong, he knew that. He beckoned the past like an invisible beast that could grind him into nothing.

He remained for a long time in dead air, eyes closed.

Until, finally, time went backward…

CHAPTER 37

He's on campus, dividing his time between here and his home lab, so he decides to pay a visit to the shared office she's allowed to use off the Climatology Lab. This office sits in a barely trafficked corridor that intersects the main hall behind the weather diorama in the main space. Few people are here on this fall Saturday afternoon. He's glad for that, since he knows the fewer people that see them together the better. He approaches her office doorway, which is closed, feeling the anxious pull he's gotten used to as he anticipates seeing her.

He stops short when a young man comes out, someone he never saw before - bespectacled, pot-bellied in a loose flannel shirt, in his 20's but with a receding hairline, bushy hair flowing off the sides. His face is pale and impassive. He gives a sideways glance at Jonathan as he passes but says nothing.

It was James Martinson!

That was who he'd seen coming out of her office.

A tingling scissored his skin. Then it felt like a hot undertow pulled him in and his consciousness tore loose to propel him elsewhere -

Who was that, he asks her. He stands inside the windowless office with its own phony weatherscape spanning the ceiling, now in almost mystically glowing heliotrope like a polar half-night.

The wall clock reveals the date and time: December 17, 2082, 1:12 PM.

Oh, that was nobody, she says, shuffling some papers on a cluttered desk.

He glances at them, an abstruse mixture of swirls, arrows and mathematical figures. She holds one page loosely in one hand as she looks over another and he grabs it from her lightly. This offers an unrecognizable topographical diagram.

He's interested in wind patterns, she explains.

The two of you work together?

Yeah. Though this guy seems to work mostly in his own head.

What do you mean?

I mean, keeps to himself.

Like you. He smiles and gives her a peck on the cheek. He's your friend, he says inquiringly.

Lab buddy. He's all right. He's smart. No folks either. We were talking about cloud seeding, which I do happen to know something about.

He picks up a sheet of paper and reads aloud, "Seeding of warm season convective clouds seeks to exploit the latent heat released by freezing, as ice crystals are created by cooling the air. This dynamic seeding assumes that the additional latent heat adds buoyance, strengthens updrafts and assumes more low-level convergence."

OK, he says. What does he plan to do?

I don't know. He's gonna tell me later probably.

You have a date?

He wishes.

Jonathan sees an artist's sketchbook on the desk as well. She's written her name on the front.

Yours?

233

We were showing each other our drawings, she says.

You never showed me. Can I see?

He flips the pad open. He sees a pen and ink drawing of a woman in Greco-Roman garb, it seems, that's startlingly elaborate and with captions in the lower right.

What are these drawings, he asks her, intrigued.

The zodiac, she says.

He sees there are no identifiable figures. He tells her, I doubt it.

She replies, On another planet, in a different solar system. Get it? She says, The inhabitants are human-like and their planet's like Earth but the stars they see are different than ours.

Her finger taps the first drawing, in his hands.

Look, she says, this is Boleria, the archer. She wounds a man in the forest by piercing his neck, thinking he's a stag. She nurses him back to health and refuses to leave his side, though he's mute from the wound.

Oh. Wonder why you would draw that.

Because I felt like it.

Not a criticism. These are unusual, original. Vivid. If I was an art instructor I'd give you an A."

I'll put them away.

No, please don't be defensive, not necessary, I'm not being patronizing. I think it's good.

Well, she says, next…

She turns the page in the drawing pad.

Excarna, she says. A woman whose abusive step-father, the king, strips off all her flesh after she runs off with her lover and he catches her. Her bare muscles turn into vines, which reach out and strangle him.

The descriptions accompany her drawings, he sees. He says, whew.

Mitcha pulls up the page to reveal the next picture, a coiled snake with a man's face.

Bolthrax, the serpent, he reads out loud.

Mitcha says, he can crawl up a woman's vagina and drive her insane with pleasure, so that she has to beg him to eat her alive from within - all her organs, until she's engulfed inside of him.

They stand in silence for a moment, looking at this unique grotesquerie.

You don't know what to make of that one. You still don't know what to make of me, she says.

No, these are amazing, I had no idea... You're like William Blake, you made up your own mythology.

Yes. Thank you, professor, like Blake. Very good. Started working on these as a freshman when I was dabbling then just kept on, like I was compiling something, some oeuvre. Though I wasn't... But I can even tell horoscopes, using this new zodiac.

No kidding, he says

When were you born, my dear?

May 19th.

She grins and flips a page.

She tells him, If you were born on that date on that planet, your sign would be Kolvex. He's the hunter with two penises. One of them is so shrunken that it can't perform, but he lets it get suckled by small animals like rodents. The other is three times the length and girth of a normal man's.

Once he gets it into women, it gives them ecstasy beyond their wildest dreams. But he himself can never be satisfied, ever, with it. So he has to keep on finding new women all the time.

The satyr figure on the page seems a sophomoric sexual caricature to him, something like a centaur with one engorged cock and one small as a child's finger.

In some way, it disturbs him but he plays along. Good sign to be born under, I'm sure, he jokes.

Your soul-mate is born under Carina, the woman who's as deep as a well.

Mitcha reveals a drawing of the counterpart female caricature, a big-breasted comic book superwoman with serpentine hair and thick lips, naked, with muscular legs spread wide, with a wispy tuft of hair above a labia of spongy petals, which her fingers splay open seemingly to reveal mirrors within mirrors.

Mitcha says, she can never be satisfied. So she's always searching. She needs to be filled up and no man can do it for her.

Mirrors within mirrors. What's real, he thinks, who really is this young girl he's looking at, who has become his lover?

Don't tell me, he says, is that your sign?

Maybe, she says.

And what's this? he asks.

Another piece of drawing paper catches his eye. There's a heading at the top in weirdly neat block print: "Attribute the social and psychological problems of modern society to the fact that society requires people to live under conditions radically different from those under which the human race evolved, and to behave in ways that conflict with the patterns of behavior that the human race developed while living under the earlier conditions."

I don't know, she says. I mean, it's a quote from somebody.

From?

An American from the 1990's or something, some radical bomber, in fact, he wrote it. If you must know.

Oh.

I get what he's trying to say.

You do?

Don't you?

Radical nonsense.

No, it isn't. Jimmy wants me to believe, I know that, and I do.

Jimmy?

He says I'm the only one who can call him Jimmy, so I do.

He looks at what's actually drawn on the paper, under the quotation. It's a crudely drawn character of a man made out of balloon shapes, inflated arms and legs and round torso, wearing what looks like a military or policeman's cap, holding a whip.

A little silly, no? he tells Mitcha.

So, an artist he's not.

He notices a murky little imprint in the bottom corner of the drawing, something like an artist's signature - but he recognizes that it's actually a skull, big-eyed and smiling.

That's how he signs his drawings? he asks her.

I did say he's also a little unusual.

So what is it you and Jimmy believe? he asks.

237

She recites, "The Industrial Revolution and its consequences have been a disaster for the human race." That's another quote from that guy, from the twentieth century, how about that? Jimmy told me. They called him the Unabomber because he bombed universities and airports. He signed his letters to newspapers "Freedom Club." People have lost their freedom, they're over-controlled, everything's just - over-organized. How could you disagree?

OK, I don't, he says.

We're not the only ones who think that now, she says, almost argumentatively.

I'm sure.

Too much, she says, everything's just too much.

He remembers her telling him, in her backyard, "I don't know what I'm fighting for anymore." So that was why, then, she'd referenced the new Druse colony, some back-to-nature experiment - there's something in its zealous revisionism, its reductionism, that compels her. She's spent time in studies on climatology mulling over things like a "hypersnake" that could transform - destroy - the planet; the ultimate mutagenesis. So she doesn't like the world as it is, or where it's going.

In the office, the bogus purple-tinged twilight sky above them feels cold and wanting, he thinks. There's sepulchral quiet when they stop speaking. Like something is just missing.

My way isn't his way, anyway, she says, breaking what he feels is a tense silence, all of a sudden.

What do you mean?

238

I mean, I know what I can change. My body is a temple, she tells him. A temple of the darkness, but also the light. That's the yin and the yang of it.

I'm not sure I follow you on that one.

Do you think that the human race can produce gods?

I would say... no.

I mean, in the way we're supposed to. Naturally. Natural childbirth. No chemicals, no science. Like in ancient times.

He thinks to himself now that her coming out of the Clark Institute influenced Mitcha in a way maybe even she didn't fully understand: that human life could be wilfully shaped at an early age into an ideal form, if only the right elements were in place. Whatever else that Jefferson Clark was, he was not a man of technology, he thinks, but a Pavlovian materialist who believed that all behavior had to have observational correlates. Babies and children could be shaped - bred to specifics It sounded like Mitcha has come up with some hybrid philosophy that has reached Nietzschean proportions.

You believe I could give birth to a god? She asks him this looking nonchalant while standing at her desk, wearing jeans and a plain red sweater with an unraveled thread at the sleeve, and poring over ordinary weather reports.

He doesn't answer for a second. He thinks of her sylphlike but still-rawboned body, drug-infused, with its cuts and bruises; its overexhilerated sensuality and its angry flailing and also its seeming fragility. All that had drawn him in, for some reason.

There are genetic considerations, she says.

239

She has no parents, he knows; literally, she was not born of a man and woman; and whoever supplied the life-stuff from which she bloomed in vitro remains unknown.

He decides to say, yes, sure, you could give birth to a god.

Her eyes grow moist. But it still has to be natural, she goes on.

Sure, he says. He falls into silence. It seems she wants to say more but stops herself. He hugs her.

It has to be someone who's proven to be smart, physically strong, and someone who already has a child, she says.

Why is that, he asks.

That child would represent a control group, she says.

Ever the scientist, he thinks, but the poor girl had lost her bearings.

His phone button taps at him. He holds up a finger to hush Mitcha. Hi, Diana, he says.

Diana says, when are you coming home? Henry wants you to practice with him, he has the new mitt.

Yeah, OK, I'll be there in a few minutes, tell him that. Bye.

He shut the phone down. Mitcha looks away from him.

So, he says, as the mood changes again, even as the fake sky above them turns ferrous, dawn breaking like a blood vessel.

So? she says. Going home?

Well... Will you see Jimmy later?

240

He and I will have another one of our little private talks soon, yeah, I told you. Jealous?

Sure, he says. But I have to go now.

She takes control by opening the door for him. OK, go, she says.

See you later.

Later, alligator.

He steps into the hallway. He doesn't want to leave her, too much seems to be unsaid, unresolved. He feels need creeping in even as he inches away, even though he knows he has to go.

Look... he begins, but doesn't finish. OK, guess I should get out of here.

You have to, she says. But Jonathan, Mitcha goes on, you have to make a choice.

What? he says, though he's heard what she told him.

You have to make a choice, that's what you'll have to do.

He kisses her lightly, despite feeling too visible in the hallway, gives a little wave then walks away, turning around to see she's already gone back inside the office.

He sat still in his car.

What he'd intuited was true. Mitcha knew James Martinson intimately, even if platonically; and Martinson was beginning to tell her things.

It had been some days later that Jonathan and Mitcha kept the tryst in the Climatology Lab, which he'd recollected on junkie island. That was the point at which he told her he'd have a child with her, what she demanded. That was the choice she was forcing him to make. That had been her plan; that was what she'd been talking about in this new

241

memory, which was so clear and complete. Maybe she loved him, maybe she didn't; but she admired his intelligence, goals, compassion and discipline. And he was the only family man she knew. Maybe the only person she'd been willing to trust in her whole life.

That was a month before she died.

Maybe he never knew what happened in the later meetings she kept with Martinson. But it seemed likely she was given a vision by him of the coming apocalypse, before she was killed - though without a chance for her to confirm it or act. Martinson killed her because he told her - he was looking for an intimate partner but she spurned him.

In her own way, also sick but unlike Martinson, Mitcha wanted life to go on, not end.

He noticed a message had come in. It was the information he'd requested from the Wright Group - the back-up file for his research plus the latest inventory before his lab blew up. This had to be released with Dr. Rose's clearance, now that there was no longer any point to keep the information hidden from him or anyone.

In a second, Cape's face came up on the car screen. "Dr. Jonathan Kelton, I order you to turn yourself in to police custody. You're under arrest for the murder of Mitcha Ebrey."

He felt a kink in his gut. Naturally, she just saw the Wright Group inventory that had suddenly become available, no longer confidential. She saw Kerosote. It was something she'd been waiting for. "No, listen -"

"I understand that you just came out of the Bluestone Clinic for medical reasons and you may be in a weakened state. We know where you are. So we'll let you turn yourself in. All right? Now! Otherwise, we come and get you and that won't be so pleasant."

"Look, please listen, Martinson did try to conspire with her. I just remembered it. It's not me, it was him! She was starting to reject his ideas. Maybe he was working alone, after all. But I think he got scared about what he confided to her, after she started pushing him away."

"That right?"

"Detective Cape, Janice, I was her friend through it all. But it was Martinson who... who..."

"Who wasn't even around," Cape said. "Don't you think we checked? It was the first thing we did."

"What? You did?" He touched the mind-d behind his ear, like picking at a scab. "Please tell me what you found out."

"He was gone for a week at a conference in Phoenix, Arizona - some tech exhibition where he was most interested in, guess what, night aerial application, otherwise known as crop dusting. The entire week from February 2nd to February 9th. It was in that time that she was murdered and her house got burned down. And all records show Martinson in Phoenix for the entire time. All right, scumbag?"

His head swam. With Mitcha out of school, out of Martinson's life, then with her vanishing so mysteriously and so completely without a word, he must have assumed she'd abandoned him. Martinson was left with nobody.

About three months later - in time for the spring clouds about which he'd consulted her - he tried to destroy the world.

"So get down here," Cape said. "Nobody's gonna fucking help you now."

CHAPTER 38

He tooled out of the campus where he'd once tried to do good, purposely slowly. He assumed he would never see it again.

So Martinson didn't kill Mitcha. He couldn't have done it, and must never have known himself what really happened to her.

In his frantic calculating, Jonathan couldn't help but think again how Dr. Rose, though he seemingly just tried to help him with the mind-d, had been a liar and manipulator, all along.

Why couldn't Rose have lied to him about his relationship to Mitcha as well?

He'd been so overwhelmed finding out about Henry that he accepted Rose acting dismissive about Mitcha. But what if that was an act?

He thought again, what if it wasn't just a coincidence that he became the subject of Rose's experiment?

How could Rose's people really have gotten to his place so fast after the lab explosion? Unless - Rose knew about it in advance.

Let Cape come and get him, he thought. He couldn't just give up, even in only minutes he had remaining.

He drove to the home of his neighbor, Mrs. Arancia. The cops would know where he was, so if they followed him into Mrs. Arancia's house then they would learn whatever she knew as well, in case she did know something significant. If there was any indication she'd seen Dr. Rose's men approaching his house before the fire in his lab, that would be damning.

When he arrived, he found the police car that had been keeping watch on his own house was gone. He knocked on the old woman's door and she didn't act happy to see him this second time. He got woozy and his knees buckled.

From the ground, he found her eyes peering into his. "My goodness," she said. "What's wrong?"

Mrs. Arancia helped him up and hurried him inside. It was inadvertent but his spell of nervous exhaustion softened her resistance. His body like rags of flesh, he lay back on her plum-colored couch. She placed a cup of tea and crackers on a plate in front of him. He bit off the edge of a stale cracker.

He said, "I'm not recovered..." He glanced through her living room window, guessing that a carefully positioned armchair chair was her unquiet lookout post. It remained an effort for him to speak. "Detective Janice Cape - you know she's investigating the murder of a girl who was once my student. Right after she was killed, there was the fire in my lab. The explosion happened so fast I don't know what caused it... Do you - do you remember the day of my fire?"

She went wide-eyed, as though she couldn't forget it if she wanted to. "Can I ask... please, did you see anything?"

"Well... I was boiling string beans and red potatoes in the kitchen. Richard's favorite. When I heard an explosion. Like a thud. I remember thinking it was a car, I thought a car blew up on the street. So I went to the window."

"Yes?"

"I saw black smoke, no flames…"

"No, the fire would've been contained within the metal walls."

"Next thing I know, the big thing, you know, the hovercraft, it's over the street, in minutes, men coming down a ramp, rushing into your house, a lot of equipment."

"How long did it take them to get here?"

"How could I know that? It was all over in a couple minutes."

"Yes… OK. Well…"

Air felt thin in his lungs. He had to face Diana now. This time, it was good-bye. He searched for the strength to get up from the couch. He said, "I was just… thinking about the time frame…"

Henry should not have come into his lab. No, nothing should have happened the way it did.

She said, "Yes, I sometimes get things mixed up myself. That's why I…"

"Why what?"

She took a moment and her expression grew darker. "Why should I tell you anything?"

So she had wanted to tell him something. He blurted out, "Mrs. Arancia, my son - my son Henry, he died in the fire."

"Oh, my. I wondered why I hadn't seen him all year. I thought it was because of the horrors." She was talking about God-zero. Then she said, "So you suffered like I have."

"Yes, I have… Please, what can you tell me… anything?"

247

"I don't want to mislead anybody, I never did. I think… it's nothing."

She appeared to be conducting a debate within herself, her thumb and forefinger rubbing together so quickly it looked as if she were trying to start a fire. He watched her stand that way for a moment, abstracted. Then she said, "The way he looked at me…"

Jonathan sat forward. "He."

"This man. He drove by, down this block. Past your house, my house too. Then he drove away."

"What're you saying? Who was it? When?"

She drew a long breath. "One day, almost a year ago, I was just sitting here, and saw this man drive by."

"A year ago? When, exactly?"

"It was, I believe, February 2nd of last year."

"My God, you know exactly? You recall to the day! Just a few days before the girl was murdered. Before the explosion in my lab. You saw a man drive by once, that's it? What are you talking about?"

"I saw a man twice… He drove past once, then again a few minutes later, like he went around the block."

"Someone you recognized?"

"No. I didn't know who it was. But - he stopped, Dr. Kelton. He looked straight at me through my window, while he was sitting in his car. Stared at me! Like he was mad I looked at him. He put up the car window quickly so I couldn't see him anymore." In what seemed an unconscious impulse, Mrs. Arancia jabbed a button on her chair and the living room window turned into a jade green sheet,

248

more like china than glass. "But I felt, for some reason, he could tell everything about me in that second."

Overwrought and paranoid, she'd locked that image in her memory and squirreled away the precise date. "And so -"

"It was in his eyes," she said. "Hate - hate for everything I was. That was what I thought. On that day."

"Hate. On that day."

She squeezed her hands together to still them. "I tried not to think about it."

"What'd this man do?"

"He didn't do anything. He never even got out of his car... You see? People would laugh at me."

"No, no, they never would."

In the semi-darkness of this noiseless room, she went on, "I didn't forget. I couldn't. HRH. There were those little letters in script on the side of his car."

"Hudson River Hawks..." Their nickname; their logo. Zachariah Willer. "Mrs. Arancia. I know who you're talking about. You - you never told anyone this!"

She seemed relieved and confounded at the same time. "Only my husband."

More useless, starved talking to the dead. "That was the dead girl's boyfriend! You didn't know that. But you're saying now that - that this guy drove past my house three days before the fire?"

"Does that make a difference?"

"Yes, it does make a difference!"

249

The difference it made was that Zachariah Willer lied to Cape. He stated under questioning that he only followed Jonathan and Mitcha once, to Tristesse. He never admitted that he knew exactly who Jonathan was, and took the trouble to find out where he lived; and then, drove by looking murderous, and looking obsessed, according to Mrs. Arancia.

Probably, he'd learned that Mitcha wanted to have a baby with Jonathan and not him.

Of course.

That was why Zachariah killed her.

"Mrs. Arancia, this is something the police need to hear. I'm going to meet them. You must tell them this!" He uttered a mechanical "thank you," leaving her with her hands clasped over her chest, as he dashed out of the home of this foolish woman who might save him.

He figured Cape would be waiting for him outside. Oddly, he saw no sign of the police.

CHAPTER 39

He sped away under the wintry roseate sky. He'd tell Cape personally what he learned from Mrs. Arancia.

So Mitcha's death had nothing to do with Dr. Rose, after all. Zachariah Willer had been the clutching boyfriend, pushed too far, what Jonathan had considered from the beginning. This had to be something the detective was willing to believe too. Mitcha's body was hidden in the river and Zachariah worked on the river.

From the car, he phoned Quinton Lent's number. Quinton couldn't extort money from him anymore, all he could do was help implicate Zachariah. He got a steady bleating sound, representing a permanently de-activated phone or one that had been destroyed.

Surprisingly, Mrs. Arancia showed up on his car screen. "Dr. Kelton, I must tell you that I did tell the police something. When they first started asking questions a week ago, when that girl's body was found."

So there was something else she'd wanted to say. But it seemed she'd been scared to say it to his face. She was afraid of everything else, why shouldn't she be afraid of him? Yet she was scrupulously honest. "What is it?"

She said, "I saw the girl. I'm almost sure it was her. The one who got killed. That day."

"That day? Please be more clear."

"I told you, the day your lab blew up, I was inside my house, I was busy. But I did happen to look out at some point during the early morning and... and - I didn't see her go into your house. It's not my concern, and I don't really know anything. I was reluctant to say anything to the police even. But I believe it was her, driving by on a motorbike."

"What? You're saying that Mitcha Ebrey drove by my house on the day of the fire in my lab too?"

"You understand that I had to tell the police. I thought you should know."

"Wait a minute..." That meant, if Mrs. Arancia was correct, that Mitcha wasn't killed on February 4 but on February 5. "Is that all you saw?"

"I didn't think anything of it. I didn't know who she was at the time, just a stranger passing by. So I went back into my kitchen."

The time frame. The time frame had been wrong...

But what did that change? Mitcha had left a message for him to meet, the very last message she ever sent. He never responded. So she tried to find him, on February 5. But he was locked away in his lab and it seemed to her that no one was home. That was possible. It was also tragically wrong. Jonathan and Henry were home. In the lab together.

The timeline regarding Mitcha's murder seemed only moderately altered with this. She was killed and her house was burned down on the same day - the exact hour of each still un-retraceable with precision. Cape knew this. It didn't mean Zachariah wasn't guilty.

"All right," he said.

Mrs. Arancia vanished from his screen.

252

He drove onto a main road not far from his house. He got bounced forcefully against the inside of the car door. Suddenly, a maroon sports coupe bearing an HRH logo was slapping itself against his moving car, like a pilot fish moving with it then veering right, ramming Jonathan's vehicle towards the edge of the road. His Ford's engine revved to a thin whine. He watched himself barreling along the shoulder of the four-line parkway, gravel spitting off the right side as the car in an impotent frenzy tried to direct itself back onto the road. He knew that in no time, with the frame damaged, the sensors in the car would give out, he'd no longer have automatic guidance.

One hand firmly on the steering wheel, he switched to manual and the wheel shimmied violently. Then, the coupe impacted his left side, walloping a fissure in the door. He caught sight of Zachariah Willer, wild-eyed, as Zachariah's car lurched back to pound into the side of Jonathan's again. He decelerated and his Ford dropped behind. Zachariah's coupe decelerated too. The coupe banged again against his punch-drunk, little vehicle - Jonathan's body vibrating as the interior quivered straight through. As they raced down the road, he saw himself only feet from a line of leafless birch trees on the right.

He fumbled in the glove compartment and whipped out the flare gun he'd seen there earlier. He lowered the car window, neck and neck with Zachariah. He fired. The charge cracked in the air and Zachariah's windshield exploded into fragments in a pinwheel of sparks. Jonathan couldn't steer properly and the Ford shrieked into an S-curve in a spray of wet dirt, several dozen yards ahead of the coupe.

No other cars were on the road. Fog dropped like stalactites from a rippled ceiling of clouds. If Zachariah chose, they could fight in this dank wilderness until one of them got annihilated.

The coupe rocketed forward, clanging as it crashed into the still Ford's front end, jolting Jonathan sideways in the crumpling interior. Then the coupe jerked backward, poised to attack him again. Zachariah was trying to crush him to death within the car.

Jonathan leaned out the window and fired again. This time, through the jagged windshield in the other car, he saw Zachariah's shoulder rupture with a starburst of blue flame. Zachariah writhed and his car, as if a horse breaking from the stall, hurtled past Jonathan. The coupe flew off the road in a wide arc, flipping onto its roof in a ravine.

Jonathan parked above the hollow where the coupe, smoldering, had enfolded itself on a blanket of grass. His own car's front tire blew out, smacking him forward inside. He shoved his jammed door open and stumbled into the smoky air towards the ravine, where the other car laid creaking and settling. Zachariah himself, horribly, seemed twisted like a screw through the middle of the frame. A blood-soaked arm punched through the driver's window. He was alive. A siren arose. Jonathan slid the rest of the way down the hill to within ten feet of Zachariah's car. It stank of burnt oil and a swampy effluvium.

Zachariah spoke, through a swollen mouth, "Mother-fucker, you... You killed her..."

CHAPTER 40

Why would Zachariah say this now? After all this!

His unmitigated grief plus the relentless beating he took in the car sapped him. His knees gave out again and he couldn't help falling to the dirt. A medical helicopter thwacked downward a hundred yards away, coming in for a landing in a clearing on the roadside. Why didn't the paramedics move in, he wondered - then realized: Zachariah's car could blow up.

Zachariah seemed to be sneering even in his upside-down agony. "She would've... was gonna come back to me."

What happened in the next few seconds was unclear to him, as he noticed a figure in a long coat out of the corner of his eye standing on the ridge above them, while, from the other direction, two paramedics ran towards him, gesticulating. A popping noise came from the heap of Zachariah's car. It caught fire. He could see the man in the wreck with a bloody hole over his eye, a gun lying under his protruding hand. Before he knew it, air rushed at him, pushing Jonathan's face into the mud, while his insides shuddered. It became unbearably hot and he rolled away. The other car enveloped itself in multi-colored flame.

Looming above him was Janice Cape in a flowing blue coat, her gun drawn, the cop shielding her eyes from the sheets of fire. In a final effort, Zachariah Willer, out of his head, had tried to shoot him. And Cape saved Jonathan's life.

State Troopers, men and women in brown uniforms, stood on the road watching listlessly as workers sprayed down Zachariah's car with foam. Jonathan sat with Cape in her police vehicle.

"Don't know how Willer thought he could get away with it," she said. "People know they're gonna get caught but we can't prevent 'em from going over the edge. Happens too much these days." She popped a small red cube into her mouth, an ordinary stimulant. "So Quinton Lent - we had him in custody. We applied a little pressure. Lo and behold, he admits he tried to blackmail you."

"He did try to blackmail me." So Cape had shifted her attention to Quinton Lent and that was why she'd pulled back on keeping watch on his house.

"Lent was greedy. I guess the blackmail didn't take with you."

"Right."

"The point is, Lent looks you up before he finds all of the girl's messages."

"Messages?"

"Lent uncovered threatening messages that Willer sent to the girl. That's why Willer delayed in reporting her missing, it seems. He was worried about implicating himself - Willer was jealous and he had sent threats to her. Meantime, after she dies, Lent, as her one living relative, is entitled to her personal effects, what little there are. So he happens to find some items she hid away on a hard drive at her adopted mother's house in Seattle. Lent finds another target besides you - Willer."

"I didn't realize."

"No," she said. "So that's why."

"Why what?"

"Why he did it. Why Willer kills him... Quinton Lent is dead."

"Dead? I just tried to reach him..."

"Willer must've set up Mr. Lent with the promise of a payday. Instead, Willer shoots him. How do you like that?" Cape looked like she hadn't slept but seemed unusually contented now. In her mind, maybe she'd won a smoldering yet strategic battle with Dr. Rose; with already-neutered media outlets; with Jonathan himself. She went on, "Quinton Lent hid away all that stuff about Willer at the Seattle house. But we found it. Now we got evidence that Willer threatened Mitcha Ebrey. It's more provable motive than you have. And we know for a fact he put a bullet in Lent. Same HRH gun he just tried to use against you. He's a killer. You, meantime, got an alibi for the time when Lent was popped anyway - you're laid up in the Bluestone Clinic."

"I was."

"Willer must've burned her house down too. As we both know, Kerosote is difficult to get but not impossible. I'm willing to believe he had his sources through HRH."

"Wow. Yes. Does that mean -?"

"Yeah, you got lucky. The arrest warrant is dropped. We can wrap this up."

His beaten body felt a little lighter. He said, "By the way, she did want to have a child. I can't say exactly why she fixated on me but she did. It wasn't with Willer. It was with me. He was lying to you about that too, or else, delusional. No doubt,

257

he found out the truth. That was why he got crazy. I realize now that was his motive for killing her."

"Yeah, that must be it."

"I just talked to my neighbor, Mrs. Arancia, she'll confirm Willer was stalking me too, she saw him come by my house. He never told you that he did. I wanted to tell you. That's where I was going just now, trying to find you to tell you."

"And so you found me."

The two of them watched Zachariah's car, a lumpy slab of metal swelling with foam like a fungus. "Look what the hell he's capable of," he said.

But there was more - there always seemed to be more. Jonathan said, "James Martinson was interested in Mitcha, I do know that. I can tell you that. And... I think she pushed him away, finally. I wonder if... even she drove Martinson over the edge."

"Listen. I wish we could dig him up and kill him five more times. We know Ebrey knew him, definitely. Maybe he even told her things. Bad things. Maybe she pissed him off. Drove him to the brink. We'll never know. But Martinson didn't murder her."

In minutes, Zachariah's car would be lifted by helicopter out of the ravine and destroyed; a corpse left within the tangle of metal and vaporized. The flooding river and contaminated soil still made local underground burial undesirable, he knew.

"You had your share, haven't you?" Cape said.

"You - do you know about - about... my son?"

"Cat's outta the bag."

"It was Quinton Lent who told you that?"

258

"That guy wasn't worth more than the drugs in his body, was he?"

So that was another reason Janice Cape felt differently about him now. She pitied him.

Cape said, "I realize that I was chasing down the wrong guy, you, partly because Rose threw up so many roadblocks. But now, I get why he did. He was hiding something. But it had nothing to do with the dead girl... He used you, didn't he?"

"Yeah."

Cape played restlessly with her fake fingers. What was she thinking about the life-changing, world-changing Henry phenomenon? She said, "You all right now or what?"

Of course not, he thought to himself; he felt he could never climb out of this pit of loss. "All right to get out of here."

"I don't know about your vehicle."

"If the engine's OK, I can probably drive it home."

"Give it a shot." She released his handcuff with a fingernail-sized chip.

The police car door eased open by itself. "Dr. Rose didn't win," she said.

She tightened her jaw and centered herself in the seat. Then her car pulled away, leaving him alone on the road.

In the ravine, the metallic remains of Zachariah's car fire beat out hissing, low notes.

"You killed her." What Zachariah said. What Cape hadn't heard.

He stared into the blaze. He still wore Rose's new mind-d. His temples stung as it reactivated at once.

259

Now a sudden, ultimate, nearly paralyzing memory…

Finally, Jonathan could remember what caused the fire in his lab. He was free to do that; his mind and body free of both Cape and Dr. Rose. He could remember what happened to Mitcha.

The device in his lab had warned him about something crucial. He realized what it was.

Unknown to Janice Cape or anyone else, Mitcha's murder didn't come down to Zachariah Willer. Nor to Dr. Rose; not to Quinton Lent or James Martinson, or some unknown stranger. In the end, it did come down to him. Zachariah was right. He did kill her.

And the truth was worse than he imagined.

CHAPTER 41

They park in the dirt driveway of her ramshackle Victorian house. A light glows dimly on the second floor, red like a church candle, beckoning them inside. He follows her up creaking steps within the house, as she takes out a key and unlocks this secret upstairs room. Eyes glazed, she bangs open the door. She wears a Victorian-looking, ankle-length black dress, with lace trimming. She also wears the gold bracelet he gave her, hiding the cost from Diana, with her initial "M."

The walls are hung with thick-linked chains, plus electric prods. There are rusty pincers. Leg and neck irons. Ugly, knotted whips for medieval mortification. Dried bloodstains dotting bare planks, familiar to him. There's a cot here as well. Someone else has stayed here sometimes, somebody he's never met - he continues to believe that though she still denies it.

Why would you think I care who stays here? he's already said. I know you have other men.

The only man I want is you, she tells him. We're going to have a baby together.

I know that's what you want, he says.

More than anything right now, she says. I want to have a baby.

She removes the taser from her pocket. He sees that she also holds a new, more powerful cartridge. One that can simulate auto-erotic asphyxiation. For later. A final high.

This is a room in this two hundred year old house, sinking on its foundations, ridden with vermin, where they've begun to indulge themselves outside of Tristesse.

Mitcha, he tells her, look at this.

What do you mean?

All this.

He opens his hands to indicate this nightmarish room. Some of her own made-up astrological drawings decorate the ceiling. Bolthrax the serpent, a sexual demon with a man's face, and Kolvex the hunter, with two mutated cocks. Like faintly twinkling constellations but the drawings are painted in blood. Her own blood. Ghastly and childish at the same time.

Jonathan says, I don't want to do it anymore.

It's what you want too, you told me that.

Her body seems to swallow him. She sticks the taser into the flesh of his belly like a fork. The prongs bite but it doesn't take long before he is subtly ravished from within. He sometimes giddily imagines it like champagne bubbles filling his head - plus, then, blood, sweat and semen streaming from his body like diamonds cutting through the hard glass of reality - suffusing it with euphoria, transcendentally sparkling!

Mitcha is like some sacred witch and all that matters is to be inside of her, which is the center of the universe.

She rakes her nails down his chest. I want it now, she tells him.

Want what? he asks.

This is the right time, I want to do it now, I can conceive now.

She pushes him to the cot, which has clean sheets in this bloody, blurry room. He feels woozy. Shackles appear in her hand.

Chain me to the bed, she says. Like we do. Then fuck me. Like we do. Only this time, it can be different. It's different.

Mitcha...

Do it. Jonathan. Please.

He thinks about it, as best he can.

Finally, he does what he has to do -

CHAPTER 42

His fault.

Back home, he found Diana on the couch, spinning a blond curl in her finger. He said, "Zachariah Willer's dead."

"Who?"

"Mitcha Ebrey's boyfriend."

"I've been asleep since we talked," she said, as though that explained something.

"Detective Janice Cape assumes that this guy Willer killed her," he said, voice straining. "Case closed."

Ice rattled as she picked up a dirty, half-full glass from the floor. "Good."

She took a slow sip of her drink and he smelled the whisky. She shuffled away from him in bare feet. He thought: maybe the truth would rise in still waters - there would be no need for more violent upheaval. "I understand, Diana, that when the men came from the Bluestone Clinic, right after the fire..."

She didn't look at him. "I told you, Dr. Rose said he could restore everything, Henry, everything... Just by chance, he already knew you - and he said he could bring our child back."

"I know what Rose told you. The problem is, Rose never knew the whole truth."

She seemed to be arguing with herself, silently. She paced.

"I know, Diana. I know what happened now."

"Do you?" She sighed. "For the first time in my life, I knew things nobody else did. I was in control. And I could put things right."

"What's right? In this case?"

"We could all be together again."

He thought back to the warning he got in his lab. He'd recalled the camping trip in the Adirondacks, only a day before that. If only he could have seen the signs more clearly. But how could he? Had there been signs?

He said, "Mrs. Arancia, the neighbor, she told me she remembered Mitcha coming here that day. February fifth."

"That old woman is batty, who would believe her?"

"I know what happened to Mitcha now." He waited a long moment. "What should we do about it?"

She looked at him squarely. "I don't know. Sweetheart. What should we do?"

"You were home. And Mitcha came in. She did come in! Mrs. Arancia didn't see that, she must not have seen it - she's scared and she watches, then she shuts out the world. But she told me that's what really happened, that Mitcha came by here. Didn't she?"

"She wanted to have a baby with you, I guess."

"She told you that?"

"Yes. She told me that you promised her!"

"Diana... My God, even though I did, I never intended to. In fact -"

"In fact what!"

"I ended it! The day before! We were together one last time. In her house."

265

When Mitcha led him to her upstairs room, on the day that she'd wanted to conceive a child, he knew, in the end, that he couldn't do it.

You will do it, she tells him.

She pushes him towards the cot. His euphoria withers. He wants to go.

She says, I told you once, if we don't have a baby, I'll leave you.

I know. There's no other way. This is a mistake.

A mistake! she cries. Her fist pounds into his chest. Then she backhands him across the face. In his drugged state, he barely feels the blows but loses balance and staggers across the room. Her knuckles come down hard on his shoulder blades and he stumbles forward into the wall. His arms flail and his elbow strikes her jaw.

But she only laughs. I love you, she says.

Then, there's no sound and no movement. It's just the two of them standing still in this room like some timeless box of decay.

What a mess he's made, he thinks to himself.

He says, I have to go back to my family.

He grabs for the door handle.

If you leave… she says.

The door squeals as he yanks it open. I understand, he says. He clambers down the stairs.

He hears the upstairs door slam behind him.

After that abrupt and almost panicked departure, he assumed Mitcha would turn to some other man.

But she didn't. She came back to him. She came here to his house.

266

Diana said, "You ended it? Then? All I knew was that when she came here -"

"What?"

"Was that you'd broken our promise."

"Our promise?"

"We'd stopped, Jonathan. Don't you remember?"

"I remember you telling me that we - we only wanted each other, after a certain point but -"

"After you caught me with that poor kid, Roger... you and I said never again. Never again. It was the way to keep us together - we would make it be just us."

"Diana... I - I wish to God I had now... that I'd been a different man. A better man. I do know that."

"Too late now... When you said you promised to have a child with her, after I realized you broke your promise to me, I just - didn't know what to think."

Mitcha's visit here was foolhardy, brazen, there could be no question of that. But it was Diana who'd become infected.

He remembered seeing himself in the home movies feeding the dribbling liquid into Henry's mouth with his finger, before the Adirondacks trip. The three of them had prepared for the night out camping. And Diana! She swilled his mosquito repellent right from the bottle...

She muttered, "My God, my God... I couldn't believe what happened."

He believed that - even in her dissociated state, she must have regretted it then. What actually set everything off anyway was a devastating aberration.

No one, not the ignorant Janice Cape, nor Dr. Rose, in his own self-involved master plan, could have known the truth. It was discovered by his secondary lab unit, which tried to warn him. It was obliterated in the fire...

CHAPTER 43

Two days after the camping trip, he works in his lab, alone, the steel door closed. He thinks that Diana is going to drive Henry to school.

A screen in the lab lights up. What he reads on this secondary unit scares him.

Before he can think what to do, the lab door is opened...

That secondary unit was intended to check and re-check data and that's what it had done. He'd earlier input that he administered his mosquito repellent to Diana and Henry, in advance of their overnight getaway to the Adirondacks. Anything dispensed from his lab, he would have made note of.

The mosquito repellent.

It had been so effective and long-lasting in general use, especially when a virulent sub-species erupted in South America, that it had made him prominent in his field. But the never-sleeping device in his lab was alerting him to something; it had hit upon anomalies, with insufficient information about consequences, in regard to his formula when ingested by people who were also taking Diana's psychiatric medication, the new drug Eufonia. Jonathan, Diana and Henry's medical histories had all been input as well.

He was being warned just at that moment that the contraindication could be extreme: there could be some profound chemical reaction. That was what he was being told: his past achievement, the mosquito repellent, in this way might even be fatally flawed.

So that night, during their trip to the Adirondacks, by drinking the liquid he insisted she take, she'd experienced a severe chemical imbalance. This formula in her body would remain active for days.

Diana suffered a psychotic break.

He said to her, now, "Please tell me what did happen. Can you?" She blinked rapidly. It seemed to him that she was searching for the right words. He prompted her. "Mitcha came here. She shouldn't have. She taunted you. You didn't even know at that point who she was. That we'd even been involved. She told you that she wanted to have a baby with me. I know that's what she wanted. But I didn't want that, I swear."

"I just wanted her to leave us alone!" She brushed back her unwashed hair. "She came in and wouldn't stop talking. She told me you always said how beautiful her eyes were. More than mine. Did you?"

"I can't... no."

She wiped away tears. "Why would she tell me that?"

"Diana!" He held her shoulders so she faced him. "Tell me!"

She pulled away from him, her hands shaking furiously. "She sent you a message..."

"Yeah, she'd left a message to meet. I only heard it a few days ago for the first time." He had to re-adjust the past timeline in his own mind. On that day, before her call, Mitcha had led him into her gruesome upstairs chamber, determined to conceive a child. Instead, he broke off the affair, left her there. So later that evening, she called him to demand a meeting. But without a response from him, Mitcha showed up at the house. That was February 5. She barged in that morning. Diana was home, while he worked in the lab. He said, "I didn't even get a chance to - to find out she was here."

"That's right, you were shut away behind that goddamn steel wall. She came here to find you but she found me first... I let her in. To find out what she wanted. I'm telling you, she went on and on about the two of you. I kept trying to stop her."

"You did stop her."

"Finally, I grabbed her by the throat. From behind. I never felt such strength before. I couldn't stop, I kept squeezing her. I wanted it, Jon. I did, I wanted to suck the life out of her. I couldn't believe what you had brought into our house! And then... she fell at my feet."

"You choked her and then you stabbed her... And then - you came after me."

The two women, in those excruciating moments, had fed each other's psychosis. For Mitcha, hers had festered in her; for Diana, it was a psychochemical reaction. After killing his mistress, Diana focused her own murderous rage - in her mind then, righteous anger - on him. In this whirlwind of destruction, she had not intended for him to survive in his lab either.

Where he and Henry were trapped.

The small amount of Kerosote he'd kept in the lab - that dose obtained through back channels for his research - lit by only a simple, slow-burning

271

fuse, would have caused a contained conflagration. "You knew I had a bio-timer there. In the lab. A detonator! I realize that now too." He'd gone through the inventory list from his lab sent to him by the Wright Group while driving here. "The Kerosote rig was a crop-gutter. If one member of a herd gets infected with a fatal disease, the whole herd has to be destroyed, I get it now, that's what I was thinking of, I switched my research to crop infestations - that's what I planned to use it for. You were a biology student once, you could figure out how to use it. You knew how to set the timer precisely, everything."

She didn't say anything, fingers tapping on her thighs. She had never lied to anyone in saying that she was out when the explosion took place. She was out disposing of Mitcha's body. All she knew was that she had to get rid of it somehow. She must have hidden the corpse in her own car in the garage. Then she drove away in what would seem an ordinary manner to Mrs. Arancia or anyone else who might happen to be looking. He could figure that the explosive timer in his lab, set for a couple of hours, would have given her time to drive to the river and in seclusion tie rocks to the corpse, wrap it in wire, taking pains to see it never rose, and plunge it into the water.

In a far-reaching lapse, there had been no ingress into their house by Dr. Rose's team, in those moments. Nor did they assume an arson fire in the lab. Their only focus was on Jonathan and mobilizing to rescue him. So Diana also had time to clean the house, quickly and as best she could. She could use her "project" to hide any possible lingering traces of the blood and mayhem. That may have been the purpose of the cathedral all along.

She could also have easily hidden Mitcha's motorbike to destroy it later, within Mitcha's own home. "What about her house?"

Diana wanted to tell him everything herself, he could see that. But however and whatever combination of trauma, relentless Eufonia use and her own chemically-induced derangement on that fateful day had damaged her, seemed to leave her flailing about for coherence and remembrance. "It all happened so fast," she said.

He knew that too: Mitcha's home got set ablaze on the same day his lab blew up, February 5. In her zeal to convict him, Cape had assumed that the fire at the house was set before his lab exploded - by him. But Mitcha's place burned down hours later.

She said, "I checked your car, I told you. So, I could find out where the bitch's house was. I took Kerosote from the lab already, when I wasn't sure how to get rid of the body. So this time, I used it to get rid of her house. I only thought of that afterward. But I didn't want anybody connecting it to you being there, I realized I had to make sure of that."

In that, Diana was simply lucky too: nobody saw her set fire to Mitcha's house, remote as it was. The time of that fire would remain inexact.

Diana said, "After Dr. Rose told me his plans, he - he promised that no one could know what happened - it had to be a secret that Henry - Henry died. So no one else would be involved. Not the

273

police, not anybody. So that's when... I knew we'd be safe."

So Diana made Rose's plan the basis of a new life.

It all might have been discovered if anyone had checked.

They sat in the heavy silence, their breathing labored.

"I know you weren't in your right mind then," he said, finally. "I do know that." There would be time later, he thought, to explain this further. "But... what you told me doesn't - doesn't explain about Henry..."

Yes, the truth was worse than he could have imagined.

He said, "Henry... he was home."

"Jon... Yes!"

"So..." He collapsed into a chair, even, felt pulled down, his energy and sanity being siphoned from him. He said, "You - Diana... I can't even imagine it... You stabbed Henry too. Didn't you? Our son?"

"Do you really remember now?"

He replayed in his mind what he'd seen in Henry's room. As Rose had indicated to him but only barely understood, Jonathan's mind-d had been at work - his conscious and unconscious minds indeed somehow became reversed when he experienced that miserable vision of his son. But that hallucination wasn't a "dream."

It was a memory.

He was being forced to relive it, literally - that he'd seen Henry stabbed repeatedly. "I do remember."

"No! Don't you see?... I didn't stab him."
"You didn't…"
Diana said, "She did!"

CHAPTER 44

The more Diana's words hammered at him, the more he recalled -

His lab door inches open.

Who's here - who would come in...?

He remains fixed on the door while the secondary lab unit flashes its warning -

What he'd imagined in Dr. Rose's white room - that it was Henry who walked into his lab - was wrong. The final moments before the fire rushed back -

Diana stands before him in the lab doorway.

She cradles the body of Henry. The boy wears pajamas, just out of bed - while he's slashed and crisscrossed with wounds.

Look at what you did! Diana tells him.

He doesn't know what she means. Horrified, he can't possibly fathom what just happened in his house.

She lays Henry's body at his feet.

Then, Diana, her arms braided with his blood, picks up a chemosterilant from a lab counter. She tosses it at Jonathan. It blinds and scorches him - sparking nerve damage and loss of motor control right away. He collapses on the lab floor. He hears her moving around but can't see and is powerless to act. He tries to crawl across the floor to do anything to stop her, to find out what has happened!

To try to save Henry, to save himself...

But he hears the lab door shut like a tomb.

That was the last thing he remembered. That he could possibly remember.

In the living room, he said, "It - it was Mitcha?"

Diana said, "I brought his body to you. To show you."

"I remember that now... The body is what I remembered..."

So that was what the mind-d brought back, if in an altered form. A nightmare and real at the same time.

She said, "Henry saw us fighting, physically fighting, in the kitchen. Before I knew what she was doing, she grabbed a knife. Henry yelled at her to stop. Then - Jon, she attacked him! She turned the knife on him instead of me. She caught him and stabbed and stabbed until he stopped moving."

"My God... So he - he was dead before the explosion..."

"Yes, he was... was already gone. The bitch killed our son."

He considered that all Diana had wanted to do then was cover up what had happened, in order to survive. She must have thought she could make it look as though he and Henry died in an accident in the lab.

The explosion set off alarm bells at the Wright Group. The medical alert from the fire would have sent out the data of the presence of two bodies in the lab. What Diana couldn't have counted on was the sudden involvement of Dr. Rose, in a sense lying in wait for bodies.

He said, "So - so you fooled Rose with your version of events. He believed Henry died in the explosion. Henry was..." His body was completely immolated.

"Afterwards, with everything that happened with Dr. Rose, I thought it was all a sign! Don't you understand? This hateful girl, this sick monster, could be erased from our lives completely! It was a sign I'd been forgiven!"

"Diana, Diana..."

She said, "Much later, I realized she must have been desperately hurt by you. She wanted what you had, which you wouldn't give her. A child... I came to believe - wanted to believe - that really, you hadn't wanted her, after all. That you got tired of her."

"Yes," he said. "I did."

When that anomalous, drug-induced state wore off, her semi-psychosis, Diana indeed must have seen things quite differently.

"But Diana, you had to lie and lie and lie..." He sat and put his head in his hands. He felt gutted.

"You shouldn't have remembered!" It was a cry of anguish not anger. "You weren't supposed to!"

He looked up, to see her holding a knife, pointed at herself. "Jon. Do it. OK?"

"No! Goddamn it, no!" He snatched the knife away from her. "No more... Please - no more! Diana..."

She collapsed into his arms and they held each other for a long time.

"I'd like to see his room," he said, at some point.

278

Subdued, she nodded yes, lying back on the couch, closing her eyes wearily, but looking somehow, to some extent, relieved.

His senses seemed sharp as ever, he gauged, as he rose and made this journey upstairs. Henry's bedroom sat undecorated and empty but for a bed, his desk and chair. Some of what he'd been seeing in his son's room for the past few days was part and parcel of the overall illusion, site-specific.

In Henry's bedroom, now, he felt surrounded by desert. He fell to his knees. Oddly, the far wall appeared to drag light towards it, as if the room became a vacuum drawing in space at a slow pace; some cosmic displacement. Then, Henry, wearing pajamas, was standing there watching him. One trompe l'oeuil after another.

"Daddy?" the boy said. "I have to go."

"What - what did I do? Henry. I'm so… so…" He mouthed the word "sorry."

Henry rose up and hovered in a heart-stopping tremolo. This made no sense. But Henry's eyes seemed soft to him. Forgiving, Jonathan told himself. Forgiving. "Good-bye," Jonathan said, softly. "Bye." Even softer.

Then Henry was gone.

Maybe it was a bizarre afterimage of the ECO-Nine hitting him or incredibly, Dr. Rose letting him experience the boy one last time. But in what felt like a waking dream state, he didn't feel emptiness. A warmth filled him, now. Somehow, he thought - wanted to think - that in the great and natural place his father had once spoken about, his son had discovered a love that was not his or Diana's, and kind beyond their comprehension.

They drove away from the house together, Diana, wordless, looking small and battered, next to him in the front seat.

She would take him to the site where she'd placed a small headstone as a memorial to Henry in a remote cemetery where no one else would know but her. Now, Jonathan would mourn him with her. What else could they do? Something would have to start over again for the two of them, somehow, though it would be in unbridgeable separateness.

In a way, Henry would come to him again, he thought. Even if he couldn't see his son - and really, didn't want to - he would believe the boy was there. In this way, he knew that, one day, he'd find his son hidden in the empty space around him; and that Henry would make it full again somehow; and unlike him, would remain safe from their torn world and complete.

THE END